A Cheating Man's Heart

Derrick Jaxn

A Cheating Man's Heart

Derrick Jaxn

First Edition: November 2013

Publisher's Note:

Website: http://derrickjaxn.com/

Facebook: https://www.facebook.com/officialderrickjaxn

Twitter: https://twitter.com/DerrickJaxn

ISBN: 978-0-9910336-0-7

Table of Contents

I was four years old when something in my father gave up on being around to see the man I'd become. Something stopped him from being proud of every move I made that resembled his own mannerisms, from swelling up with pride when people told him I was his spitting image. I learned an invaluable lesson the day he never came back, and that is that nobody deserves the feeling of having someone they love to stop loving them.

*For that reason, I dedicate this book to my father, **Winston Earl Jackson**. I love and forgive you.*

Prologue:

Every child has a super hero they want to be when they grow up. But what happens when his decisions earn him the perception-turned-reality of being a villain?

What happens when that villain finds a reason to change at a time he's not ready to? Does he cower under a sentencing without a right to a fair trial or give the vain efforts of righting his wrongs even though someone else's heart is on the line?

Because in the end, everyone feels better about having someone less than to compare themselves to. It's how we solidify our position outside the circle of judgment. But in some way or another, we are all alike. Admitting it may surrender your pride, but it also opens up your heart and allows you to remember what it feels like to not deserve a second chance.

Family Matters

It was about 5 a.m. on a Thursday morning. The sun was still asleep, and I wasn't. I had an appointment with a therapist in two hours that I had been waiting for all week. The only reason it took me so long to get the courage to go was for fear of making the front page of *See I Told You He Was Crazy* weekly magazine. Ever since my big break in the writing industry, my every move was calculated by the drama leeches aka media; the good moves divided and the bad ones multiplied exponentially. It all equaled to the price of fame.

Eyes half closed, I plopped onto the hardwood floor to do my morning routine, 200 pushups, 200 crunches, and a brief heart-to-heart with the Lord. Then I stood up to check the mirror, curious if my hairline had done any receding while I was sleeping.

The motion detectors cued the stereo to start singing *Get Down On It* as I brushed my teeth like they were the very strings of Kool and The Gang's base guitarist. At 25 years old, I had already entered a mid-life crisis, trying to catch up on the golden day of *real music* grown folks preached about.

I got dressed and pointed my keys toward the driveway to start up the Challenger, better known as Daisy Duke. She was about all I had to make me feel special. We made the other guys jealous, but so long as I was the one opening her doors, she was coming home with me every night. Fully loaded, automatic, black matte paint job; she was a beauty. And this morning her remote starter kept me from sitting on her frozen leather trying to defrost my body along with her windshield. Now that's real love.

I pulled up to the therapist's office 20 minutes early to see she had arrived only a few seconds before I did. She was walking from her car carrying two cups of coffee, a laptop bag, and biting her purse strap to free up a hand to twist the key.

"Hey, let me help you with that," I said, walking up to her.

Her facial expression was more alarmed than pleased at my offer until I got close enough for her to make out my face.

"Mr. Fletcher?" she murmured through her teeth, still using them to hold on to her purse.

I grabbed the coffee and her laptop from her and said, "That's me."

"Wow, I had no idea you were coming. The appointment was under a completely different name, a female's if I'm not mistaken."

"That would be my assistant. She booked it for discretional reasons... *if* you know what I mean."

"I understand. Well, all right, come on in."

We walked to the back through what seemed to be a maze. She was also young, late 20s-early 30s, very attractive, rocking a Stella McCartney pea coat and red-bottom heels. I didn't see a ring on her finger, probably a result of guys being too intimidated to marry a woman who earned more money than them.

"Right this way," she said, holding her office door open.

I set her things on the desk and looked around. It was decked out. Looked like something out of a furniture store catalog and over in the corner I could see the couch where she had earned her living faking empathetic nods to the life stories of complete strangers.

"Mr. Fletcher, I apologize for the unprofessionalism. I hadn't really had a chance to prepare the notes for our meeting today but if you want, we can go ahead and get started."

"Yeah that's fine, whatever works. I didn't get your name?"

"Oh, right. I'm Dr. Holley, but if it's easier for you, just call me Jesica."

I reached for a handshake. "All right Jesica, nice to meet you. I'm-"

"Shawn Fletcher. I know."

"You can call me Shaw-"

"I prefer Mr. Fletcher," She said sharply.

"Or Mr. Fletcher. Whatever works for you."

"If you will, go ahead and have a seat. You can hang your coat up behind you and take off your shoes if you want. Get comfortable."

I went over to the couch, found a sweet spot, and lay back.

"You watch a lot of TV Mr. Fletcher?"

"Not too much. What makes you ask?"

"Because I can't think of another reason why you thought it'd be acceptable to put your feet on someone's couch other than seeing it done on television."

I turned to see her looking over her glasses, smiling to see if I would too. "I'm sorry, I ain't mean nothin' by it. You said get comfortable so I was just-"

"I'm kidding, you can keep them there. Just a little joke to help my clients loosen up a bit. So now that that's out of the way, let's start by you telling me what brings you here."

I shifted in the seat, trying to keep up with her. She was switching lanes from business, to dry humor, and now back to business like she was weaving through traffic with a full bladder.

"Well-"

"Oh, by the way. I have to let you know that my sister and I are huge fans of yours. I love your blog site and poetry. You're very talented."

I put on a flattered face, hiding my thoughts of wondering whether or not this was a good idea.

"Thanks, Jesica. That means a lot."

"Oh, you're welcome. So, tell me. What brings you here?"

"Well, I've been-

"That one article you wrote about the girl who was raped by her supervisor. Heart breaking and beautiful at the same time."

"Um, thanks."

I paused. Waiting to see if she got it all out of her system before I wasted any more breath.

"Go on. Tell me why you're here."

"Well, I've been doing some thinking. A little too much actually, and it's keeping me from being able to sleep. I'm pretty sure it has something to do with my ex. Not sure if I should try again or let it go for good. Probably need to forgive myself of some things first but-"

"Things like what?"

"Like my past. My infidelity."

"You mean you cheated? *The* Shawn Fletcher was a cheater?"

I knew this was a bad idea.

"Yes, I was. And now I'm just trying to-"

"Can I ask you a question?" she interrupted again. Apparently, therapists were falsely advertised to be good listeners.

"Sure, why not?"

"Well, I don't mean to be rude, and please don't take this the wrong way. But if you were a cheater, then why do you write about relationships and love? I mean, that's kind of ironic, don't you think?"

"Well I guess you can see it that way. About as ironic as a person who's HIV-positive advocating for safe sex." I said cynically.

She cleared her throat and looked away, embarrassed. "I'm sorry, Mr. Fletcher, I hope I didn't offend you."

"Not at all. I get that question a lot. But who better to learn a lesson from than someone who's already learned it for you, right? I mean, I'm not saying I know everything, but if what I do know helps people, then I don't have a good enough reason to not keep them from making the same mistakes."

She nodded her head in agreement. "Right. Well, I like to start my sessions with the client opening up about their past. We've touched on it but I really want you to go into detail."

She propped her laptop on her knees in full documentation mode. "Tell me about yourself starting from the very first time you encountered love-like emotions all the way until your most recent. Particularly about your experiences with infidelity."

"Everything?"

"Yes, everything. Even if you think it was just puppy love. We're all the result of our experiences and to fully understand what you're dealing with now, I'll need to know what you've been through. And if you can promise to tell me everything, the complete truth, then I promise not to judge you no matter what. Deal?"

"Deal. But I have one request."

"What's that?"

"Can you please stop cutting me off?"

She looked down at her screen flustered. "I apologize Mr. Fletcher. I won't say another word unless you ask, I promise. The floor is all-"

"I'm just kidding. That was just a little joke I use to loosen up my therapists."

She looked at me and smiled, still not saying a word, honoring her promise.

I turned and looked back at the ceiling, closing my eyes, trying to think back to the days I first found love. It had to be in my teenage years, somewhere in the early 2000s.

Yeah, I could hear Momma's voice ringing through the house like it was yesterday.

"Boy, if you don't cut that damn music down! The bus will be here in a little. You need to hurry up and eat this food or I ain't cookin' for y'all no more. Try me if you want to!" she yelled. She was in the kitchen banging around pots and pans, making sure we didn't take for granted the fact that she not only went to work, but took the time to cook before she did.

I said, "All right, I'm comin'," carefully controlling the tone of my voice so that my talking loud enough to be heard wasn't confused with *talking back*. When you're a teenager, that mistake can earn you restriction from anything that rhymes with 'fun'. For the parents who liked to keep it simple, it may just get your butt whooped.

"And don't forget to write down the email of all your teachers. If I find out it's not the right email, I'mma know sum'n." She said walking down the hallway toward my room.

8

I'mma know sum'n is a black parent's translation for "The description of what I'm going to do to you could be used against me in a court of law, so use your imagination on just how physically uncomfortable I'm going to make you with the use of a belt or switch weaponry."

I said, "You got it. I'll even get their finger-prints in case you need to verify the scene of a grade that's too good to be true."

I was so nervous for the first day at my new high school that I was detailing the bottom of my sneakers. Being *first-day-of-school fresh* was like the 11th commandment. Anything less, and you pretty much wore a scarlet letter the rest of the semester.

She came and leaned in the doorway smiling. "Well, no grade is ever too good to be true. Those children gettin' straight A's don't have two brains, so there's no reason you can't do the same thing. You're smart. You're handsome, and if you keep ya head on straight, you'll get a good job one day. Maybe help me pay off some of these credit cards I ran up tryna feed ya greedy self." I started blushing. It always made me proud when she acknowledged my abnormal appetite. Something about it made me feel like a man.

"Now, I love you, and I want you to have a good day at your new school, meet some new friends, but stay away from them fast-ass girls." She walked in and sat down beside me. "I'm serious, Shawn. I don't need you bringing no babies in here and most of 'em probably got VD anyway with the way these kids actin' up."

"All right. I got it. No babies. Check."

"Now come here and give Momma a hug. I gotta get dressed for work and you'll probably be gone by the time I'm done."

"All right, Ma, I love you too. I'll see you when you get home."

She walked back out and I finished my shoe detailing. I went out of the room, pleasantly met with the aroma of scrambled eggs and smoked sausage. I was used to fending for myself in the morning with a bowl of cold cereal so the rarity was much appreciated. I fixed my plate to the unwelcomed sound of the school bus' squeaking brakes. It arrived perfectly off time and I had to stash my breakfast in a plastic grocery bag to eat on the ride to school.

I was 15 years old, the baby boy, and recently merged into a new family. I grew up with just one parent, my momma. She was the prototypical modern day black woman; strong, independent, and a connoisseur of how to discipline your kids. With multiple jobs at once, a lot of headache medicine, and cooking expertise that no culinary arts degree could teach, she singlehandedly raised four out of her five children down in Elba, Alabama.

My oldest sister wasn't ready to leave Yonkers when Momma decided to move us out of the city so my grandma agreed to keep her before she passed. Even though Momma had to play both parental roles, being the breadwinner usually took priority over her softer side of being a nurturer, but never to the point where I had to second guess her love for me. It was for that reason that I became a momma's boy, ready to take any "Yo momma" joke too seriously, no matter the time or day.

After 11 years of being approached by men who didn't cut it, she finally found somebody to settle down with; We called him Mr. Macklin. He was the old school type, worked all day and came home hungry. His upbringing was something like you'd see in *The Color Purple*. Not big on education, but prized work ethic as the true judgment of a man's character.

He went to church every Sunday, occasionally led songs for the men's choir, and had his own business. I respected that about him. Even though he was a workaholic, he always made time for the Lord. Well, that and a few beers after church for football Sunday, but who am I to judge? I liked him.

Being the new kid at school earned me much of the spotlight, particularly from my 10th grade classmates. I thought I was doing a pretty good job of disguising myself as normal by buying shirts that swallowed me, and pants six sizes too big(that was the *style)*, but every teacher took it upon themselves to blow my cover, starting the class with an introduction of the new students.

As if the classroom wasn't awkward enough, the cafeteria was like a zoo. The entire school in one big room without supervision, and no one had anything better to do than to pick out what didn't belong and stare holes through it. I felt like the new Jordans on their release date at the mall; Everyone was looking, pointing, and whispering when I walked by.

I didn't realize how uncomfortable I'd be in a new environment, but minding my business was my game plan on making it through the day.

The cafeteria food smelled delicious, and with my metabolism, I could eat to my heart's content without wearing a single love handle. I was piling up my tray with goodies when out the corner of my eye, I could see a girl trying to make eye contact with me. I took a brief glance to confirm and then turned my head back to my food but not before she received her cue to come over and introduce herself.

"Hey whasup? You the new guy everybody talking about. I'm Brittney, nice to meet you," she said reaching for a handshake. *Everybody was talking about me?* I was curious as to what was being said but more curious where this introduction was headed.

"Well, next time you see *everybody*, tell 'em I go by Shawn." That came out way smoother than I expected. I met her hand briefly so she wouldn't notice my sweaty palms.

"Well, nice to meet you, *Shawn*," she said sarcastically, stressing the pronunciation. "If you want, you can sit at our table. We got room."

"Thanks, but I got someone saving me a seat already. Maybe next time." I was lying like a champ. In high-pressured situations, my survival instincts taught me to lie first, think later. That came from growing up trying to get out of trouble when Momma conducted her interrogations to figure out whose ass had her belt's name on it.

"Oh...okay. Well, I guess I'll see you around?" she asked rhetorically as she walked off. By her tone I could tell she wasn't accustomed to hearing *no,* and understandably so. Brittney was as pretty as any girl that ever looked me in my eye...in real life. *Don't judge me.* About 5'2", curvy, fresh perm, straight teeth, and eyes that squinted when she smiled so she looked half-Asian. Typically, these girls were reserved for the popular or older guys. A scrawny, goofy-looking underclassman like myself was used to being on the outskirts of attention. I even made it my home. So of course, all it took was a little hospitality on my first day for me to feel like I had met my soul mate.

From that day on, I saw Brittney what seemed to be everywhere, and every time she gave me the little spirit finger wave. Spirit fingers are to teenage boys what smiley faces at the end of text messages are to teenage girls; I was whipped. By the end of the first week, I had mustered enough courage to ask her for her number. The tricky part was trying to catch her when she wasn't with her herd of nosy-ass friends. The only thing worse than getting shut down by a girl was getting shut down by a girl in front of more girls-social suicide.

Over the following week, I had gotten Brittney's schedule memorized. She went to her social studies class first thing in the morning, always early so she could get her seat at the front with no problem. She took her break at the end of the hallway that led from the gym so her and her crew would be the first thing the basketball team saw on their way from morning shoot-around. After that, her math, English, and economics classes were back to back with only lunch in between them on fourth hall with the rest of the 10th grade classes. Her last class got out five minutes earlier than her friends which was plenty for me to *coincidentally* bump into her after she came out the classroom so I could make my power move.

"Hey, Britt."

"Oh, hey, Shawn, I didn't know you had class on this hall too."

"Oh, I don't. I was just tutoring students for a math class today. You know, trying to help out when I can." There went those trusty survival instincts of mine again.

"Well, that's sweet of you. But I thought tutoring was always after school. Did they change it or something?"

"Yeah, well, sorta. Look, I don't want to get off subject. I have a question," I said, panicking.

"Okay what is it?" When she asked that, it seemed as if the entire hallway got just quiet enough to eavesdrop on our conversation.

"Umm. Well, I just wanted to know if, umm..if you have a piece of paper I can borrow."

"Sure, is that it? You acted like it was something really major. I almost thought you were going to ask for my...never mind. Here you go. All you needed was one sheet? I got plenty," she said, flipping through her binder.

"Wait, so what did you think I was going to say?"

"Nothing, it's silly. Forget about it," she murmured, handing me the sheet of paper.

"Say it."

"No, I said forget about it."

"Well, what if I asked you for your number? Would you give it to me?"

She paused a moment to see if I was serious. "There's only one way to find out."

"Okay, so can I have your number?"

"No, you cannot."

"So why didn't you just say that in the first place?"

"Why didn't you just ask in the first place? Besides, I don't give out my number, but you can give me yours and maybe I'll call you." This was my first lesson on how complicated girls could be. Luckily, I came prepared with it written down, already folded, and in hand.

"Here you go. I guess I'll talk to you later then."

"Yeah, you guess," and she walked off.

I wasn't sure if that was her way of letting me down softly, but I couldn't fight the optimism from her not being grossed out by my attempt. You couldn't tell me shit. I walked away feeling like Bruce Willis with a fiery car explosion behind me as Aerosmith's *Don't Wanna Miss a Thing* played in the background. Whether she called me or not, I had arrived.

Contrary to my luck, she did. By this time, my cool had worn off, and I was back to being the nervous and inexperienced me I had always been. I wasn't sure what to say on the phone, but I went through the basic, "So tell me a little about yourself" spiel you'd see in your average Tyler Perry movie, and it worked. Brittney was a preacher's daughter, the lead singer in the church choir, and a straight A student. Sexy, smart, and filled with the Holy Spirit. *Bingo*. I wasn't quite the saint, but I always felt guilty for my sins at church, and then started backsliding Sunday evening when I got pissed off again; you know, your average Christian. Our relationship with the Lord was our common ground, so much that we even decided to have our first "date" at church. Where I'm from, having a "church boo" meant you were serious. I was already far ahead of myself, so a few more steps wouldn't hurt. This church date was my proof that our feelings were now mutual and you couldn't tell me any different.

A couple weeks went by and things were going great. We hung out at school and on the weekends at church. With no car, early curfews, and parents who found any reason to complain about gas, the 15 minute long drive between our houses meant we were in a long distance relationship.

Both of our parents were strict but for different reasons; Hers wanted to keep her on the straight and narrow; mine wanted to keep the phone bill and babies to a minimum. So we snuck on the phone every night around 10 after they went to bed, said a prayer to ask God to forgive us of our disobedience, then talked until we fell asleep.

Most of it was just ramble about how much we couldn't stand to be without the other. Occasionally we'd get off subject to something of substance. But one thing was for sure, I was in love with a nice girl, going to church more often, and it felt good. This new school thing was working out quite well.

I stayed up one night gazing out the window, wishing I was brave enough to climb out of it and meet Brittney somewhere. Not sure on how I'd get to her, but in my imagination, there were no rules. Hell, I could even fly if I felt like it. I wanted to get a small rock and throw it at her window, let her come and open it up to see me dressed in a tux jumping up and down and waving my hands.

But with my luck, I'd get profiled by one of the policemen on night-patrol who saw the small rock in my hand, got trigger happy, and sent bullets flying in my direction for being *armed and dangerous*. After all, I lived in Alabama and a lot of rednecks were still being sore losers after the civil war. So I snapped out of it; tried to think of something a little more realistic.

There was far too much pinned-up infatuation I needed to do something with. Usher was singing *You Got it Bad* from the alarm clock radio over on the dresser, and I knew he was talking to me.

I was no R&B star like him, but with a poem, I wanted to sing Brittney the same song to let her know how I felt. I could give it to her the next day when we passed our morning notes before class. We kept it basic with our love letters since text messaging was new and still on the come-up back then.

I got up and turned on the lights to find some paper and a pencil. I didn't know where to start with the poem; trying to establish my manliness while expressing my feelings showed me why guys my age were typically looking to be the next MJ or Lil Wayne. But I didn't have a jumper nor cared to be a rapper, so I just started writing:

Roses are red, violets are blue.

Nah, I'm just kidding. Because both of those are half truths.

'Cuz if you see a rose in the right spot you'll see that they come in different colors

And violets are black sometimes, just ask Stevie Wonder.

Okay, you know I'm just kidding. But hopefully it made you smile.

'Cuz that's all I want for you, even if I'm not around

to see it.

You needed a good brother but your ex couldn't be it.

So you lost faith in us but I'mma give you one more to believe in.

To prove to you we not too young to know what love is

I wanna show you enough till you know what too much is.

Forever's not long enough when it comes to the time we spend

but if you let me, I'll use it to be your lover and your friend.

I promise.

Short, sweet, and to the point. I spell checked it one time, then folded it neatly into a square. She loved thoughtful gifts like this. All that was left now was to hand it to her.

So, I put it in the clear sleeve of the cover of my three-ring binder. I was rightfully a little paranoid about losing it. I could lose the ground if I didn't have it to walk on; especially in the mornings when I was practically a zombie. I barely even tied my shoes, just tucked the laces in and kept it moving. Lazy, I know.

I woke up the next day to the tune of Momma's morning bedroom door pounding as usual. Got up a little easier this time, excited to pick out my clothes for the day. It was a special occasion so I wanted to spruce it up a bit. Pull out all the stops.

One thing I knew about girls is that they could always appreciate a mature guy, and Brittney was no different. I looked in my closet, rummaged around a bit. Found some dress clothes I hadn't worn in a while that were still in good shape.

The GQ magazine guys looked fly in their dress shirts, but all of mine swallowed me because Momma didn't shop for our clothes to fit; she shopped for clothes to grow into. They lasted longer that way, but I needed mine to fit so I could look like Denzel and 'em.

My creative juices started flowing, and I found my way to a few safety pins in the bottom of one of my drawers. Figured tailoring a shirt couldn't be that difficult; I already knew the look I wanted. Just had to pull the shirt a little more snug to my body and keep the pins hidden.

After about 30 minutes of nipping and tucking, I had done the best I could do. The shirt looked more like sails on a ship with the shirt sleeves dangling freely while the breast of the shirt was pulled snugly to my bird chest and balled up in the back. My pants were still a little on the baggy side, but it hid my chicken legs so I wasn't tripping. In fact, I was proud.

I grabbed my books and went out the room, but just for reassurance, stopped at Alvin's door. I knew he'd tell me the truth.

Alvin was the 15-year-old spitting image of his father, Mr. Macklin, and was older than me by six months. By looking at us you'd think he was the younger step-brother. I was a little above average height, but he was a bad posture away from being a dwarf. He didn't talk much, just stayed in his room drawing cartoons and watching wrestling all day. I never could figure him out. He always seemed really shifty. At times we were "friends", and other times exactly the strangers we had always been before we met.

I was the complete opposite. I loved playing sports, had a slight obsession with PB&J sandwiches, and was never too mature for a good prank. Before Mr. Macklin came along, Momma ran a tight ship when it came to wasting electricity, so I knew how to find ways to entertain myself that didn't include video games, cable, or anything else that affected the light bill.

I heard his cartoons blasting through the door. He usually briefed himself on the latest episodes so that his friends wouldn't catch him slipping in the debate about which Dragon Ball Z character was the next to die.

"Ay yo, Alvin. Can I come in?"

"Hold on," he said. I could see him through the door not doing a damn thing other than watching TV. "Okay yeah, come in."

"Ay bruh, I just had to see what you thought about the fit. I'm tryin' sum'n a little different today. Tryna be on my grown-man tip. This straight or I need to change?"

He paused the TV, surprisingly, and walked up to me. It dawned on me that I had no business asking him anything about fashion. His dad had programmed him to "the cheaper the better" type of mentality when getting clothes so his taste was all based on the best deal.

"Turn around real quick one time." He examined me like the expert he wasn't. "Hmm...I say keep the shirt and pants, add a hat and maybe some glasses to bring out the look and you're good to go."

"Okay, a hat like what? Like a top hat or-"

"Come on, man, nobody wears top hats but old folks. You need you a Kango or sum'n. Daddy got a few of 'em and he already gone for work. Just grab one from his closet. He ain't gon' notice."

"Oh, okay then bet." I set my books down and went into their room.

Nervous as hell, I ran into their closet and flipped on the light. Their room was like sacred ground and we were just mere sinners. If I got caught, I wouldn't hear or feel the end of it.

I found Mr. Macklin's hat collection hanging from the inside of his door. His precious Kangos were right there, live and in living color. I grabbed the black one and turned the lights off. It was a universal color, so I was told, and went with everything.

I looked on his dresser for some glasses and saw something even better, cologne. I didn't have time to smell each one so I picked the sleekest bottle and started spraying my neck. Didn't smell it enough so I sprayed a few more times on my shirt, wrists, and behind my ears. Had to make sure it'd last the whole day.

I came back out and heard the bus pulling up. I went into Alvin's room to grab my stuff, but it was gone. He must've grabbed it and taken it with him.

Panicking, because missing the bus was a great way to stitch your name on Momma's belt, I flew out the house, shirt sleeves flapping in the wind. The rest of the kids saw me running and stopped the bus driver from pulling off.

I got on and made my way to the back where the other high-school kids sat. Alvin was sitting down chilling without a care in the world.

"Bruh, why you ain't tell me the bus was here?"

"I thought you heard it just like I did. My bad."

"Yeah, whatever man. You got my books?"

"Yeah, they right here." he said handing them to me. We didn't believe in book bags. Those were for children. A part of the induction of being a high school student was to make sure you carried your books so that your high school subjects would show on the cover. They were badges of honor.

I sat down and noticed the other students cutting eyes at me. I guess they had never seen a young brother in a Kango looking like a movie star.

We pulled up to the school and Brittney was being dropped off by her parents. She went to public school against their wishes, but they weren't budging when it came to the transportation. The lack of supervision outside of what a bus driver could see in his rear view mirror scared them to death of how much *normal* the other kids could infect their precious baby with.

She looked good. Damn good. Her hair was laid, as usual, neatly parted down the middle as if Moses himself had done it. Her sundress was wrapping around her curves and stopping just short of her freshly manicured toes.

"Whasup sweetheart?" I said, trying to catch up to her. She gave me the 'I see you but my parents are still watching, so be cool' type of look.

We walked in the double doors and shared a hug.

"Hey, babe," she said, smelling my neck. "Is that cologne you got on?"

"Yeah, you like it?"

"My nose hurts."

"What you mean? It stinks?"

"No, I mean my nose hurts. I feel like I just poured it in my nostrils. Why'd you put so much on? And what are you wearing, boo?"

"I'm just tryin' a little something new. You like it?"

She shifted. "I mean, I guess. It is...different. It makes you look older. Much older."

"Well, thank you, I thought you'd notice," I said smiling big enough to light a room.

The warning bell rung, letting us know we had five minutes to get to class. We both scrambled around for our morning letters to hand to one another. I grabbed my notebook and looked to the cover.

The poem was gone.

I checked around my feet to see if I had dropped it.

"Here, take this, I gotta get to class," she said, trying to hand me her letter.

"Ugh...hold on. I got yours too. I just gotta....find...where I put...it." I looked in the binder. Nothing. I checked in my text books. Still nothing.

"Well, it's okay. Just give it to me later on."

"Aight." I grabbed her letter as she turned and hit the morning shopping mall speed walk down the hall that elderly people are known for.

I knew I would lose that damn poem.

I was thinking about it all day, wondering if anyone picked it up. I didn't put a name on it, which may have been a good thing too. Knowing the kids at our school, that poem would've been scanned and uploaded to Myspace in no time.

I could give it to her the next day, but no way I was about to put in the same work to look and smell good too. Maybe it was bad luck. Seems like when you try the hardest, things find a way to go wrong.

I got home later on and went straight to my room. Didn't feel like being bothered. I had suffered through stares and side chuckles at my outfit all day and it was all for nothing.

A few hours went by and Momma and Mr. Macklin got home from work. I heard them laughing about something. Loud. The kind of laugh where your stomach hurts and you only take a break to breathe. I had to know what was so funny and plus I wanted to inquire about when dinner would be ready.

Walked out my room and saw them huddled up around the dining room table. Alvin was there too. They all looked at me and got silent.

"Roses are....red," Momma chuckled. "Violets. Violets are blue." Then they busted out laughing again.

I looked on the table and saw what they were all looking at. My poem. It was there, freshly unfolded and the center of attention.

I was livid. "What'chal doin with that?!" I went over and snatched it from under them. They ignored me and continued their laughs without even breaking stride. I looked at Alvin. He was the only one making eye contact. It had to be him.

"Bruh, where y'all found this?"

He shrugged his shoulders and said, "We didn't find it. It was in my room. You left it."

"Wait, you went in my binder? Dude, what the hell is wrong with you?"

Momma's face snapped tight. "What did you say?" Then she got up out of her chair and rolled up on me. I got a little frightened but still had some anger left to stand my ground.

"Momma, that was wrong, and he knew it. That is my property. He had no business taking it."

"I don't care what he took. Don't you ever let me hear that come out your mouth again, you hear?"

"Yes, ma'am," I said, exhaling in the back of my mind. Normally she would've already been swinging. I guess even she could understand somewhat.

Alvin was still on the other side watching in amusement. I wanted to explode, but he'd like that too much. I went back to my room and carefully closed the door. Not because I wasn't mad; I just knew I was on thin ice after my slip of the tongue.

I took the letter and ripped it to pieces. Balled it up. Un-balled it. Separated it into three portions. Balled it up again and threw it in the garbage. I didn't want any chance of it being read again by anyone.

I couldn't wait for 10 o'clock to roll around so I could finally talk to Brittney again. She was about the only thing that could bring me out of a bad mood. I wasn't about to tell her what happened because chances were, she would've started nagging about wanting the poem and I'd be right back at square one.

Then I heard the door open and Mr. Macklin barged in. My parents, like most black parents, were strong advocates in the absence of our privacy so long as the roof over our heads was in their name.

"Boy, whatchu doin?" he said in his deep Southern accent coming through the doorway. I hated being called *boy* but I knew it came from a good place with him. Besides, that had been his greeting since the first time we met. Consistency was his forte.

"Nothing much. Just looking at some notes from class." I lied. I just wanted to give him a valid reason to leave me alone.

"Well, I didn't wanna both' ya. But ya momma told me to come in here and talk to ya bout ya lil' girlfriend at the schoolhouse. She supposed you done got stung by the love bug and might need a lil' advice 'bout scratchin' the itch."

I didn't know where the hell he got his phrases from, but I assumed that was his way of trying to connect with me. I gave him a pass for effort, but the generational gap was never so evident as it was at that moment.

"She's not my *lil'* girlfriend, Mr. Macklin. We're a couple now, and yeah, you can say we're pretty serious."

"Well, whateva ya wanna cawl it, there's a couple thangs you needs to know befo' you do something you gon' regret." While not at all sure where the conversation was headed and definitely skeptical about his relationship coaching credentials, what could I say? This guy pulled my mother so he must have known something.

"Now I was yo age once, I know how it is. Dese lil' girls runnin' around in they lil' skirts and they wants to flirt and all this and that. I know. But you can't neva trust nothin' dat bleed for sem' days and don't die."

This was, in fact, my *Birds 'n' the Bees* talk after all. He had yet to enjoy the pleasure of a heart-to-heart with his chip off the old block about girls since Alvin was so busy obsessing over anime drawings, so I guess I was the next best thing.

"But Mr. Macklin, you married Momma. Don't you trust her?"

"See me, now dat's different. I'm 40 years old. It was time for me to give up on awl'at. I had my fun already." As if marriage was doomsday and every day since was another treacherous step on the green mile. "You don't wanna be like me. Ya young, ya got plenty mo lil' girls that's gon' come ya way, and you don't wanna be tied down yet. Sew ya oats till you ready to stir the pot or you gon' ruin the breakfast for everybody." he said and he walked out.

Don't ask me what he meant. I was just as confused as you are. I just knew that for the first time, I finally had found true love and I wasn't giving that up for anyone.

Six months went by and my relationship with Brittney was flourishing. She was the number-one friend on my Myspace Top Eight and our picture was each other's background. We were finally able to go out on real dates so long as her mom waited out in the parking lot.

She even came to the house a few times and we held hands flipping through channels, sneaking in kisses. Had to stay in the living room, of course, which got annoying because everyone looked at us when they walked past, but it was better than nothing. We were in love.

One day out of nowhere, Alvin decided he had found love too. Up until this point, I was the only one using the phone so I had it whenever I pleased. He knew he'd be imposing on my phone time but he didn't care. He just walked past me one day and said, "Hey, man, I'mma need the phone tonight too."

Asshole.

Even though I had started hanging out with Brittney after school, the phone was the corner stone of our relationship. That's where we bonded the most. It was our getaway. We came up with little questionnaire games, picked out lyrics to our favorite songs to dedicate to one another, and everything else first time lovers do. But with Alvin's little stunt, our happily-ever-after was already being thrown a curve ball.

I couldn't afford to have him go snitching to the parents, especially with Brittney and I already sneaking around after curfew hours for the phone. So, I negotiated a deal that would allow him to use the phone until 11 p.m. and I'd have it the rest of the night.

This way, if Brittney called right at 11 before Alvin finished his conversation with whoever he was already on the phone with, she'd quietly beep in instead of ringing every phone in the house, allowing us to do a smooth transition on some *Bourne Identity* shit. Neither of us were happy about sacrificing an hour of our precious quality time, but our hands were tied and Alvin had no problem pulling that knot unmercifully tight.

This worked for about a week, no problem, but then the extra hour lapse started to take its toll on us. She became too tired to talk as long as we used to before drifting off, and with less communication came other problems like the blame game, arguments, and feeling distant.

Although things weren't the same, there was still no question that my heart had made itself comfortably at home. But that wasn't enough to keep our relationship from hitting a plateau while my step-brother was bumping shoulders with cupid. His conversations were spilling over into my time, but the more Brittney and I were at each other's throats, the less I tried to stop him.

Emotionally, I was in waist deep. My love was the kind of love that they showed in the R&B videos, but there was no slow motion walks through fields of flowers, no standing outside throwing rocks at the window, none of that.

Finally, I came to a decision; Brittney and I were going to have a conference with the Lord so He could put us back on track. The preacher told me I could do all things through Christ, so surely rekindling that flame was within His grasp. It was a desperation move, but the desperate times called for it. My next conversation with her was going to be with Jesus on the phone. No arguing, no fussing, just prayer.

Night time came and Alvin was doing his usual, taking too long and spilling over into my time despite the fact he had been on the phone nearly four hours now, since eight o'clock. His notice to get off the phone was usually a light knock at the door, but I was in one of those pranking moods.

One thing we always feared was Momma picking up the phone, telling us to hang up her *damn* phone before she came in there and did something creatively violent. That subtle "click" the phone made when it was picked up was as distinct a sound as hearing the car pull up when you know the house was still dirty after your parents told you it better be clean when they got home.

I was in the middle of puberty, but I could still imitate Momma's voice to a T. If I did it right, Alvin would have no problem hanging up the phone fast and in a hurry, and I would have no problem laughing about it.

I went into the kitchen, cleared my throat, picked up the phone and before I could get anything out, I heard Brittney's voice, "Aww, Alvin….I love you too."

My Brother's Keeper

I immediately hung up. My heart pounded so hard I could literally feel it in my chest. My knees gave way and the wall behind me broke my fall as I slumped down to the floor. I thought I knew my worst nightmare, but this far exceeded any fear I had fathomed till that point.

Trying to make sense of it all without overreacting, I considered all possible scenarios. The only one I could think of was that the girl I loved, the first girl I ever loved, just told my "brother" that she loved him.

Hypnotized by the repetitive memory of that moment, I lay there on the floor as I felt my heart shatter piece by piece. It was an out-of-body experience unlike anything I had ever felt.

About 30 minutes went by, and I heard Alvin's room door open. He walked down the hall and caught me lying on the kitchen floor. Casually he stopped short in the dining room and put the phone on the couch. "Hey man, Brittney's on the phone. It's all yours," he said as he non-chalantly walked back to his room and shut the door. I felt a mixture of being lost and outraged all at once. I sat there a few minutes and then gathered myself enough to walk over to the couch and put the phone to my face.

"Hellooo…Shaaaawn? Are you there? Say something," she said in that exact same voice that was now playing on repeat in my mind.

"I can hear you breathing, Shawn. Why aren't you talking?"

I sat there a few more seconds then hung up. I didn't know if she'd try calling back or not, but I figured if she did, she'd just get a very unwelcoming message from my mother which was fine by me. I couldn't wrap my mind around what all had taken place in those last few moments, and on some level, I didn't want to.

I tried to find every excuse for what could've happened or how she could've meant it. I checked the phone for a possible explanation, maybe there was an eerily similar-sounding girl Alvin was speaking to at the very moment I picked up the phone.

I picked up the phone and scrolled through the call history. There were no dialed calls, just one received call at around 8 p.m. when he first got the phone and went into his room, and it was from the number of the one girl in charge of my heart. I went back to my room, shut the door, and opened the window for ventilation.

Sleep was out the question, so I sat up against the headboard, motionless. Too much was happening at one time and the person I'd normally talk to was the very person causing it all. Little did I know, this was only the beginning. Hour after hour, I tuned out of real life and just took the punishment. They say what comes around goes around, but never did I imagine what I could've done to deserve this. I didn't know who to blame, so I blamed God. He's in control, so why didn't He stop this? I asked him for a girl, and this is who He sent. But why did He do this to me? I wanted to talk to Him too, but I figured He had to be mad, and besides, He never responded anyway. It was just me, my sorrow, and my memories until the sun came up. Some would say it was just puppy love, but the torture of coming to reality was very real. This was my first heartbreak and it was as advertised.

Once the sun was high enough to turn off the street lights, Momma's door opened and she made her rounds banging on our room doors.

"Wake up, wake up! You know the drill!" she yelled walking to the kitchen to start her coffee.

I was still awake, tears dried up and crystallized on my cheeks. I was so unsure of everything at this point that even looking in the mirror was an unfamiliar sight. I wanted to go in there and fight Alvin, and I'd most likely win with the way I was feeling. But that'd surely start some commotion between Momma and Mr. Macklin once he got involved to stop it or start defending his son. I definitely didn't want that.

Knowing Alvin, he'd go back to school bruised up, and when people asked him what happened, he'd say it was because he "stole my girl". Embarrassing to say the least, figured I'd pass on that too.

I'd just keep my distance until I decided what to do with him. We weren't the best of friends anyway, so what'd I expect? For him to still respect the fact that we were now calling each other family? Guess not.

As for Brittney, I knew exactly how I wanted to confront her. Face to face. Our last conversation ended in dial tone, but I still doubt she had any idea we were over. But before I made that clear to her, I wanted answers.

I got dressed for school, purposely getting out the house last-minute so I wouldn't have to stop and talk to anyone. Since I was horrible at timing the bus, I had to just listen for the squeaking brakes and next-door neighbor's kids yelling to their siblings to come out . Our bus driver was one of those who was doing what he had to do to make ends meet. He made it clear by the look on his face every morning that he was no happier to see me get on his bus than I was to be getting on it. But neither of us had a choice.

I manually took every breath as I walked into school, hoping that pacing myself would calm me down. It was as crowded as Wal-Mart on Black Friday. Students hustling around trying to go to the cafe before class and others lobbying for people who did their homework to let them plagiarize.

My locker was on the far side of the school forcing me to push through countless book bags, endure the morning breaths of those who didn't see hygiene as a worthy priority, and overhear conversations about whether or not the rookie sensation, Lebron James, would be the next Michael Jordan. A few people spoke to me on my way, but I only saw their lips moving, and nodded back. I could hardly concentrate on anything outside of my thoughts.

When I finally got to my locker, Brittney was there, arms folded, eye-brows furrowed, hips cocked to one side. Normally she'd be with her flock of friends until we coordinated a place to see each other in between classes. Just the sight of her felt like electricity shooting through my spine. I had suppressed my emotions enough to keep it together until then, but they were getting ready to break through like floodwater through a levy.

"Umm..you hung up on me last night. What's your problem?" she said as her neck rolled from side to side. Without warning, tears began filling up my eyes. I tried looking away but one dropped too soon.

"Baby, talk to me. What happened?" she said now sounding concerned.

That was the straw that broke my back. I slammed my locker shut so fast her hair flew. The sound caught people's attention around us and I could see them tuning in to the show.

"Why?! I don't understand…just…how could you?! He's MY FUCKING BROTHER!!" Before I knew it, I was yelling and she had backed up to a safe distance. Her face changed from an *it's on* attitude to *oh shit* fear in a matter of seconds.

"Shawn, it's not what you think. I-"

"Don't give me that shit. It's exactly what I think. I just wish I had *thought it* sooner before I got with your trifling ass."

"But you not even letting me explain. Like, I really didn't mean to keep it from you. I just-"

"Accidentally never mentioned it when we talked? Every day. Right?"

"Well, yeah, I mean no. I mean I was going to try to tell you eventually once the time was right."

"So when is the time right to simply not have something to tell me? When is the time right to not fuck around with someone's own family. Someone who they have to see every day and night because they live in the same house."

"Shawn, you know I would never purposely hurt you like that."

"Someone who's eating at the same table every day. Getting on the school bus together every day. You know, I was foolish enough to believe that if you were to ever do something so stupid as cheat on me, it wouldn't be with my own damn brother I have to see every *damn* day."

"He's not your brother. He's your step-brother."

The crowd harmonized an "Ooooh," and I could feel my hands clenching and the veins in my temple pulsating. My blood was like lava but my heart became ice cold.

"And you're not my girlfriend, just some bitch that couldn't resist the opportunity to let every guy in the school have a piece of you, no matter how they're related."

"Shawn, you know I didn't mean it like that, I'm just saying-"

I was already 10 steps past her before her voice was drowned out by the sound of the school chattering again, psychoanalyzing everything that just happened like a Super Bowl instant replay. They all parted as I went through it, eyes fixed on me and recording my every move.

I was glad I left because there was no telling what I was about to do next. I never before had felt anger like I did then, and mixed with the embarrassment of it happening in front of the entire school, my actions were becoming vulnerable to the very hostile moment. I knew I could never look my mother in the face knowing I had put my hands on a female regardless of the situation. But breaking someone's heart while blatantly disrespecting them is a good way to tempt a young man who's used to learning his lessons the hard way.

I went to a bathroom on the other side of the school, found a stall, and locked it. I needed a chance to break down so I could mellow out. Her voice was still haunting me with the repetitive memory of "Aww Alvin…I love you too" now coupled with the visual of the caller I.D. showing her received call at 8 p.m. That shit hurt.

The rest of the school day was a blur, and by this time everyone had gotten word of what had happened at my locker. All of a sudden complete strangers were coming up to me, asking if I was okay. Not wanting to be bothered is like fresh blood to annoying ass sharks. The day you don't feel like talking is when people try their hardest to make you speak up. Just as they tried to set me up to get the spiel, I'd knock ém down with a rude and blunt dismissal.

I thought I'd never make it home, but when I did, I indulged in a music binge. When no one else knows how I feel, R&B does. Interrupting my thoughts with a heartbreak playlist was exactly what I wanted, and exactly what I didn't need.

I was spiraling down memory lane with old pictures and love letters, having my "Dear God, why me?" moment. I prayed, slept, and cleaned, but the entire time all I could think about was how nothing was what it seemed. The first time you question one person's love, you question everyone's love, and that was the scariest moment of being at rock bottom.

After a few days of missed calls from Brittney and unnoticed silent treatment to my family, I still hadn't gone very far from square one. I was stuck in somewhat of a numb state. Lucifer himself could've jumped out from under my bed and I wouldn't have batted an eye.

My mind was a hamster wheel of question marks: How could she? How long has it been going on? What now? Answers I would never get on my own listening to '90s slow jams. Brittney was calling regularly every two hours, and I was ignoring her on the same rhythm.

After a while, I grew a little weary of the curiosity of what it was she could possibly have to say that was giving her confidence I'd entertain it. So I picked up.

"Shawn…Shawn, is that you?" she said trembling. Even she sounded surprised I answered.

"I just wanna know why and for how long. That's it," It was a little weird for me to take this tone with her, especially knowing she was probably crying. That had always been my soft spot, her tears, but that soft spot was frozen and dipped into *never again* cement.

"I'm sorry, I didn't mean to-"

"Tell me why or I'm hanging up."

" Okay don't hang up…please." She gave a defeated exhale and then began to confess. "It never was supposed to be anything serious. Things just didn't feel the same between us, and I started having questions about how you felt. You…I don't know, you just didn't seem like you were interested in me like you used to be. I started wondering if you really had to call me later because of your brother or if it was something else so I just asked him myself. He told me that you were telling the truth and then we just started talking about you and then it went from there. We ended up talking more and more every night and feelings came out of nowhere. I didn't plan it and I don't think he did neither. He made me feel how you used to, the

35

nice things he said, the way he thought about life, how he would alw-
"

"How long ago?"

"Uh…umm I guess maybe like a month or so. Not long after you said you'd have to start calling me a little later in the evenings."

"And not once did anyone wanna fill me in?"

"I mean we didn't do anything. It was just conversation. I never kissed him or hung out with him or anything, I promise. I'm so sorry. I know I was wrong but we can get past thi-"*Click*.

I had heard more than enough. I couldn't believe she had the nerve to justify it all because they didn't physically hook up. Hell, I didn't know if I believed that either. As far as I was concerned, she was somebody I thought existed; just a figment of my imagination and love was in the same category.

I was cold, and had all intentions on remaining that way. As for my "brother", I had to admit where we stood. Surely he knew that I found out what'd been going on, and he had yet to come out and talk about it. Honestly, he didn't owe me anything. Not an explanation, not honesty, and not a friendship. But if he was on fire and I had a cup of water, I'd drink it. Slowly. With a straw. That would sum up our brotherhood from then on for all I cared.

It was time to move on. After Brittney finally got the message that it was over between us, she felt free to explore whatever it was her and Alvin had going on. Neither one of them spared their public display of affection in school, and it was the talk of the 10th grade class. It was easier to pretend I didn't care rather than admit it was killing me. Sometimes it's the people you'd give the shirt off your back that are the first ones to stab you in it. Lesson learned.

As a teenager, your insecurities become the laws of attraction. I never before realized my narrow shoulders, lack of muscle mass on my 5'10", 160 pound frame, and how huge my feet were. I was the only 15 year old I knew whose shoe size matched his age.

I wasn't old enough to get tattoos nor interested in the thought of them. I didn't need my name branded on me to remember it and on my dark skin, a design was more likely to turn out like a silhouette.

Still determined for an upgrade, I went outside and got Mr. Macklin's old rusted weight set out of the garage; it was not only a health hazard, it was damn near a booby-trap. There were spiders everywhere and screws were missing in the bench so it always felt like it was going to tip over.

As trifling as it was, it became my own little distant island I could escape to nightly to purge energy that would've otherwise been spent over thinking. Night after night, I kept going faithfully. Lifting more, and weighing more, becoming addicted to the feeling of being physically superior to my former self.

By my 12th grade year I had put on 60 pounds of muscle, and stood at 6'4. In a society obsessed with physical appearance, this not only changed me, but it also changed everyone around me. I was no longer just the new kid at school. I was officially in the upper echelon as a jock.

Jocks had life easy. More girls, more handshakes, and probably the best thing was the look on my ex's face when she saw me with my new girlfriend of the moment. Love was out the question. I played the hand I was dealt and I was winning. Despite all of that, my life felt like a brand new engine that wouldn't stop leaking, and I didn't know how to plug it.

One day I was cleaning up and ran across a box of love letters from Brittney. I told myself to just trash it and keep it moving but like always, I didn't listen. I figured it wouldn't hurt to just take a peek before it was gone for good. Like clockwork, I was right back listening to my *Since You Been Gone* playlist trying to figure out where it all went wrong.

There was no way I could go through the rest of my life with loose ends, but did that mean I should reach out to her to tie them? No. I'd rather tea bag a bear trap. I learned my lesson about handing out my heart.

That moment, I made a conscious decision to start becoming a man. My own man. It was time that I finally got to know life on a first-name basis instead of just through word-of-mouth. It was time for me to clean my slate and leave for college.

Me, Myself, and...Damn Who Is That?

From my first step on the campus of Tuskegee University, nothing was the same.

There were people from all over the world with different personalities and backgrounds. Being that it was an HBCU, the one thing we had in common was our race with the exception of the one white boy in band and the madly in love couple from Spain who played on the tennis team. Other than that, there were a lot of new faces waiting to be met, but I was still on a mission to get to know me first.

I decided to become spiritually in tune with myself. I always had a relationship with God, but I could never quite get a handle on Christianity. No matter how many times I fasted, sat on the front row at church, sang along with the choir, abbreviated cuss words and repented when they slipped; something about me never quite got it right and I got tired of asking questions no one had answers to. Like who King James was and why we should trust his version of the bible. I wasn't expecting the pastor to provide me with his résumé, but I thought it was fair to know a little about Mr. James' biography. His favorite colors. Something.

After asking so many questions and getting the same answer, "Pray about it.", I decided I could do that from my dorm room with Joel Osteen smiling on my little TV that sat atop the mini fridge. At least there, I knew it wouldn't be a collection plate passed around four or five times while I got the side-eye for plucking the bottom to make it sound like I made a deposit.

Besides, the guilt of giving into my flesh did more to distract me than help me find myself. So I made peace by agreeing that if God gave it to me, then there must've been a reason for it. I figured it'd be better to find out the reason the hard way, than to die and never know at all.

So, it was time for my hormones to experience emancipation at its finest. To do so, I followed the Single Man's Code of Conduct(SMCC); a little something I invented to maintain ethical responsibility while I was having my fun.

The SMCC consisted of 10 rules:

1. Never have unprotected sex. Wrap it up, strap twice, pull out early, morning after pill, water hose it down afterwards. You can never be too safe.

2. Never tell any secrets of your past. That's when you're forced to trust.

3. Never go out on dates that are in broad daylight, nor show you were thinking about her. Completely generic dinner and movie dates are allowed but that's it.

4. Never give or accept gifts from the heart. Those are tiny investments of love that you never notice until everything's ended and it's time to get rid of them.

5. Never answer calls before booty call hours. Otherwise you'll position yourself as someone who's there when needed.

6. Never allow tagged photos on Facebook. If this rule is broken, they must be blocked and ignored for some other unforeseen reason you're too emotional to discuss.

7. Never use words like "beautiful", "amazing", or "special" to describe what you think of them. Those are danger words when it comes to the heart.

8. Never tell the truth about what's on your mind. You'll indirectly rely on them to care and if they do, you're screwed.

9. Never meet her friends. They will catch you doing something. You can't avoid that. When they do, you need to be able to say they don't know you.

10. Never allow feelings room to grow. If for whatever reason they slip in, you have to cut it off.

If there was a right way to be single, this was it.

Sure, from time to time there were drinks thrown in my face, but so what? Even a dead clock is right twice a day. Mine, maybe not so frequent, but it worked for me.

Girls came and went like a revolving door. They would accept the terms of agreement at first and then later ask the infamous question, "So...what are we doing?" I'd reply with "What you think? The same thing we do every night," and of course, it never went over well, so they moved on to the next man. The last thing I was doing was losing sleep over keeping my heart a priority. My circle was tight, I trusted people's actions over their promises, and I was no longer apologizing for who I was. Things were finally going my way.

While I came across a lot of pretty faces, there were none quite like Jazmin. She was cut-throat, a little hoodrat, and funny as hell. Long, expensive weave, curves to live for, and a walk like Tyra, even in flats. Jazmin was that Mary J. Blige back in the '90s type of chick that every man desired, even if for one night.

She did a little urban car show modeling in high school before she moved from Atlanta. Had dreams of going mainstream but didn't like the idea of nice hips being misconstrued as "plus-sized". So it was either the stripper pole or student loans. Luckily she got a scholarship.

We had amazing sex, a lot of it. Still young, but old enough to know what to do and brave enough to try more. We pushed our bodies to the limit, almost got caught a few times, but played it off and tried again later somewhere else. The only thing between our sex and perfection was the lack of emotion. We were friends, but both of us were determined to prove how little we could care about the other. The way I wanted it.

My entire freshman year, I had my team led by this down-ass female who wasn't ready for a relationship, every bachelor's dream. But like most, I hit the snooze button one too many times, and Jazmin was giving me the "we gotta talk" talk before I knew it.

"It's not you, it's me," she said. Blunt without so much as the courtesy to pretend she cared.

"Wait, what you mean it's over? I thought we were just, you know, chilling. You can't break up with me if there's nothing to break."

"Oh, but I can and I am."

"Why fix it if it's not broken? Where is all of this coming from anyway?"

"It is broken. I don't wanna be ya placeholder pussy any more. I'm ready to settle down and actually try the relationship thing."

"Relationship? Look, if it makes you feel better then fine. Be my girlfriend."

"Boy stop. What I look like? For one, I don't want you, and two, I have somebody that wants me more than just part time. Run that shit on them other chicks you be dealing with."

"Oh, so now you better than them?"

She cut her eyes at me.

"C'mon Jaz, you being dramatic. Okay, look. We can stop the sex, but let's at least be friends. For real this time, just friends." I gave her the puppy dog face. I didn't really care about being 'friends'; I just wanted to stay in the picture in case things fell out with her new guy. Classic technique.

She curled her lips and rolled her eyes."Aight. We can still be cool, but don't get fresh because I really like Lewis, and I don't wanna mess this up."

"Wait, you're going out with Lewis? Basketball Lewis? Word on campus is he's a jerk."

"Well, he's not to me. Long as he's not playing me, I'mma stay down for him." She shook her head affirmatively like she was agreeing with herself.

"You down with his money. Everybody knows his friends ain't his friends. They are his red Camaro with the Lambo' doors' friends."

"Has nothing to do with his car. I mean it ain't like I never been in a Camaro before. It takes more than that."

"Okay whatever. Can I still come over for dinner though? I don't even have to stay. You can leave it by the door when you done and I'll just come pick it up." We both started laughing even though I was partly serious. She could cook her ass off and I'd be damned if I gave up on the hot plates that easy.

I had a feeling this all was just a cry for attention anyway. Yeah, I was that narcissistic. As far as my sex life was concerned, the show must go on.

I got in my first class of the spring semester and all of my classmates came back looking fresh, wearing everything on their Christmas list. I sat in my usual seat towards the back with the rest of the in-class text messagers and exam whisperers, prowling for new talent to add to my team.

I looked to the door and saw a prospect walking in. Her stride was a little awkward, almost dorky, but she was cute. Hair was natural textured into a neat bun, and she had slanted eyes. A little on the classy side with her attire, but I've never shied away from a challenge. Sometimes, girls will try to throw you off by not showing cleavage or calling attention to themselves but I was no rookie. I knew the game and I knew it well.

I ran a full background check on her by the time she sat down and I liked what I saw. On the front of her binder were some professional photos of her; one with a saxophone, the others more along the lines of Wal-Mart catalog ads with her smiling on a swing set and what-not.

This one was going to be interesting, and I couldn't wait for class to let out. When it did, I wasted no time.

"Hey, wha's good ma." I said with *that look* in my eye and a half grin. She paused long enough to give me the *Who the hell you talking to* face and proceeded to pack her books. But I wouldn't be defeated that easily. I had work ethic.

"I'm sorry, that came out wrong. I meant to say, hello, how are you, Danielle?"

"Do I know you?" she said with an honestly curious expression, waiting for a response.

I was in.

"Well, no...I mean not yet. But I was hoping to-"

"Then how'd you know my name?"

It wasn't supposed to go like that. "Well, unless you write your stage name at the top of your paper, I figured Danielle would be you. Are you like a model or musician or something?" I said, looking at the pictures on her binder.

"No, well, not the model part. Those are my senior pictures from high school, and I play the saxophone in my free time."

She played saxophone. That was different. Can't say I had anybody that was musically gifted on the roster. It was time to change that.

"Well, Danielle, I don't play any instruments but I'd love to hear you play sometime. Maybe we can get together outside of class and you can show me a thing or two?" I said, raising an eyebrow suggestively.

She rolled her eyes and walked off. I think I had her sold until the last part. A little too strong.

That encounter stuck with me the rest of the day. How she was able to resist my charm so effortlessly baffled me. My résumé was solid; tall, dark, handsome, in shape, my own car. It was no Beamer, but at 18 years old, I wasn't doing half bad.

I had on my fitted shirt that day, and if my breath was stinking, I'm sure someone would've told me. What was her problem? Maybe she had a man and was pretending to be faithful. A little reverse psychology to trick me into respecting her.

They say you win some, you lose some, but I just lost one in Jazmin. I wasn't about to let this one slip through my fingers.

The next day I went to plan B. I wore another fitted shirt, this one a size smaller hugging tight into my armpits, did a few push-ups, sprayed on the smell-good, and had my mustache freshly lined up. The peach fuzz on my chin was a work in progress so I left that alone. I cherished every strand I had.

I went to class late so she could see me walk in as I did my best *Obama after the Osama's Dead Announcement* strut to my seat. There was even an ocean side breeze and Shaft theme song playing, or at least that's what it felt like.

"Sorry, I'm late," I said to my professor. "My puppy looked a little under the weather so I rushed her to the veterinarian and refused to leave her side until I knew she was all right. It won't happen again."

I got a few giggles from my classmates, but the only thing between my math professor and Korea was a green card, so I doubt she understood what I said. She gave a generous smile, nodded her head, and went on teaching.

I looked out of the corner of my eye and saw Danielle. By her lack of reaction I could see she missed my introduction, but I didn't panic. There was plenty more where that came from.

I had set the tone, but now it was time for the real show. My *Teacher's Pet* routine deserved a patent for how effectively it could make any slacker look like a hard-working A student. Only three simple steps to follow:

1. Look up at the board, count to 20, mouthing each number so it looks like you're following along then put your head down to scribble approximately two to three seconds. This is the attentive note-taking technique.

2. If you see someone's hand go up, raise yours shortly after but before they get called on so that when the teacher finally gets to you, you can just say, "Oh never mind, that answered my question."

3. Repeat as necessary.

Oh yes, the players may change but the game remains the same. I was Kobe in the fourth quarter, and I'd be damned if I was passing the ball. I followed the routine to a T, didn't miss a beat nor look to see if she noticed. I knew she did, and of course, she was impressed.

Professor Kim dismissed class and it was time to reap the benefits. I turned my head to Danielle's seat to see her gone and halfway out the door. *Shit, not again* I thought. I never chased a girl in my life, but I was about to bounty hunt this one because I went through entirely too much to not even be dignified with a rejection.

I grabbed my books and rushed out behind her, keeping a safe distance so I didn't blow my cover. My only chance to get her to stop and talk was if she took the elevator. Sure enough, there was a crowd already squeezing in so she went flying down the stair-case.

I had to think fast.

"Hey, Danielle, wait up, you forgot something!" slipped out my mouth. I was brainstorming for another lie to follow up with so I wouldn't seem like a creep. I tapped my pockets, felt my answer. "Your pen! You forgot your pen." I yelled, reaching it out to her.

She didn't even look at the pen. "That's not mine. Besides, everyone knows not to use an ink pen in a math class."

"Oh okay. Well, listen, I think we may have gotten off on the wrong foot yesterday. I wanna make it up to you."

"I'm sorry. Who are you again?"

"I'm Shawn... I talked to you yesterday after math class."

"Oh yeah, I remember now. *Mr. Show Me a Thing or Two*. Look, I'm in a rush, I have to go. Excuse me." She turned away and left.

Plan C, D, E, and F went out the window. I broke character and said, "I just wanted to know if maybe we could talk sometime. I think you're really pretty."

She took a few more steps. Stopped. Then turned around. Slowly she began walking back towards me and with every step she sped up my heartbeat. I wasn't quite sure if she was reconsidering or if I really pissed her off this time and was about to get assaulted.

She looked me in my eye as if she was searching for something and said, "You know, that's probably the first genuine thing you've said to me so far."

Embarrassed and impressed at her ability to see right through me, I just kept looking at her. I felt vulnerable.

"Well, don't just stand there, ask me for my number. I don't have all day."

"Oh..um...right. Can I get your number?"

She looked at me with a motherly disappointment

"I meant, may I have your number......please?"

"Yes, you may." she said triumphantly. She grabbed my phone and put her number in. "I'm going to be late to my class because of this so you better use it." And then for the first time, she smiled.

Game Changer

Jazmin was bouncing up and down. "So you'll never guess what happened! Lewis got me a promise ring today! Look!" She held out her hand for me to see.

"Promise what?"

"Promise that we'll always be together even when we're apart"

"Wait, so then what's a wedding ring?"

"That's different. This is just a promise ring. Stop being a hater. I think it's cute. Shows that he was thinkin' bout me."

"Ain't nobody hatin', I just don't see the point. You've known the dude three weeks and he already got you acting brand new."

"I mean, yeah, but that may not be a bad thing. It feels good to know I'm on his mind. I feel comfortable being a girly girl with him, like I don't have to always be so tough. He really cares about me. I think I'm in *love*." She stared back down at her hand, glowing with felicity.

"In love? You trippin'. But whatever. I mean if he was all'at then why his last girlfriend let em go?"

"Well, they were together for a while, but then the guilt of not being good enough for him began to eat at her conscience. So she broke up with him. He was really tore up about it for a while, but he knew something would come along better, and here I am!"

If I ever smelled bullshit before, there was no doubt I was stepping knee deep in it at that very moment. But there was nothing I could tell her. He paid for her dinner, let her tag him in Facebook pictures, held her hand in public, and all this other crazy stuff that only people in relationships do. Just didn't make any sense.

"Well aight, good for you. Or congratulations? I mean, whatever. I'm happy for you. Look, I gotta go get my seat before my professor locks me out. I'll probably see you later on."

I walked off to my next class, still thinking about the news. I didn't know how to place the feeling. It wasn't necessarily jealousy, but more territorial. I had lingering hope of getting back to my flings, and this guy was making his stay less and less temporary. Promise rings. Respect. If he kept that up, she was never going to come back. Secretly, I was hoping it didn't work out, but I tried to play my position and be supportive.

We had convinced him I was like a "brother" so it wouldn't raise unnecessary suspicion. But it wasn't fair being the "other guy" without having "other guy" perks. I was lying and plotting to chill with Jazmin for no reason and getting nothing out of it. At least not what I wanted.

Until that point, I hadn't mentioned my dealings with Danielle to Jazmin. No particular reason. But the more I thought about it, the more it seemed like an opportunity to make her jealous. If not jealous, I could at least prove I wasn't tripping over her and her new lover. Even though I was. Hell, on some level, I was trying to prove it to myself.

Later that afternoon, I pulled up to Jazmin's apartment and saw her car there. The door was normally open for anyone to just walk in, but this time it wasn't. I knocked a few times, waited, knocked again a little louder, and then put my ear to the door. I heard some thumping noise against the walls and faint moans. Yeah, it was a bad time. Either she was faking or he was drastically better than I was because she sounded a lot different than what I remember. I guess that was when I realized it was over. My main sex buddy was officially gone.

I went back to my apartment, flopped on the couch, and turned on the TV. Animal Planet was showing a cheetah in pursuit of the family dinner, and it reminded me of how I had to chase Danielle that day. Why couldn't she just cooperate like other girls and pretend I caught her off guard while making it obvious she wanted me?

I went into my phone to find her number but then I caught myself; it had only been a few hours since we met. If I texted now, I'd come off thirsty. Girls love a guy who doesn't care enough, at least that's how it seemed. I guess they can't want for attention they already have because as soon as they get it, they go to acquire more from someone who's not giving it to them.

I had some homework due the next day, so I did my due diligence by making sure my other chicks were aware that it was time to help me out. By *help me out*, I mean do it and have it printed and ready to turn in by the morning. So long as I kept them sexually satisfied, they kept the good grades coming.

Without having that on my plate to think about, it just freed up mental space for Danielle. She was a new breed, and I needed a completely different game plan going forward to deal with her.

I got tired of waiting so I went ahead and texted her; waited a couple seconds, no answer. The more I waited the more I couldn't imagine what else she had better to do than to reply to my text. Once again, I broke the code and did the unthinkable. I called her, but this was an emergency. She needed to hear the unsettling in my voice about her behavior. I wasn't having it.

It rang at least six times before she picked up. I could tell by her voice that she was very comfortable, not breathing hard, or showing any other signs of rushing to the phone in case I called. Some nerve she had.

"Hey, wha's good? Why you ain't answer my text?"

"Is this Shawn?"

"Yeah, this is me. But answer my question. Why you ain't-" *click*

She hung up. Where the hell did she get off? I had to call one more time to make sure it was an accident, and if she hung up on me this time, I was deleting her number out of my phone and taking the L.

Phone ringing.

I heard her pick up and then silence. So I spoke first.

"Hello? Danielle?"

"Yes, this is she. Hi, how are you Shawn?"

Was this some kind of mind game? I thought. "I'm good. Is something wrong with your phone? It just hung up on me last time."

"My phone is fine. Your tone wasn't. You don't call people just demanding stuff, at least not my phone you won't."

"I'm sorry, I got a little ahead of myself. I just wanted to know why you didn't answer my text message," I said, now finding myself using more of a proper accent for some reason. It came out of nowhere.

"Well, I saw it, but I was finishing up my homework. Besides, some things are just better when you wait for them."

I felt her smiling through her voice. She was a step ahead of me no matter what, sometimes literally, but I could keep up. I couldn't put her in the rotation with the rest of the girls, but I liked where things were headed. Not being able to predict what was next all but satisfied my curiosity.

We went back and forth for hours. She was everything I didn't expect: humble, funny, and single. She came from a wealthy family and was raised in the suburbs, unlike myself who grew up on a dirt road and didn't even have cable until 10th grade. She had only been in one relationship that ended mutually instead of in flames like in my past. She wasn't damaged or poisoned by society's image of a "bad bitch" and how she should aspire to be one. Danielle was as wholesome of a girl as I had come across outside of my own sisters. Normally, I can spot personality flaws from a mile away, but hers were well hidden. I could've worn Ray Charles' glasses and still saw that this one was special.

I woke up the next morning wanting to pick up where we left off, but that would require a good morning text first. After the first time of talking to someone, you're never really sure if the impression is mutual, and I wasn't about to put myself out there to be shut down. She may have been unimpressed with me and already decided that the first conversation we had would be the last. Maybe she didn't think much about it at all and would act like it never happened.

Either way, I was still anxious to go to math class to find out and walked in to see she already had beat me there. She met my eyes with a welcoming smile. Didn't expect that. She had a vintage natural hairdo, something like Janelle Monae. White blouse and khaki high-waist pants. She didn't have on any make up but the lip gloss was confirmation that she was putting in a little more effort which I appreciated. Either she woke up feeling good or had me on her mind, and I conveniently assumed the latter. When I saw that she had used her books to save the seat beside her, my insides did the electric slide.

"Well, hello there. Don't you look lovely today? What's the occasion?" I said, looking for a confession of my unrelenting presence on her mind when she woke up.

"The occasion is that I'm alive and healthy. I try to look my best every day, but I can see I've fallen short by your tone."

"Oh no, I'm not saying that. You looked good before. I'm just saying that you look especially good today." Why do girls have that ability to turn any compliment into an insult? It's like we need a disclaimer before we can even be nice.

"I get it. I was just kidding. Take a joke."

" Oh okay. Is this seat for me or-"

"Yes, it's for you. I figured you were going to be late again and didn't want you getting stuck in the very back where you couldn't hear the professor. You do know that's where all the slackers sit, right?"

I was offended.

"Hey, nothing's wrong with being a slacker. They work hard to not do anything so that people like you can shine. Give them some credit. You need them."

"Oh whatever, I give them two years tops. Whoever it is doing their work for them will eventually find real boo's to do work for and they'll be so far behind that they'll get frustrated and fail out of college. And if they're playing sports, their grades will drop so low they'll be ineligible and won't have enough to pay tuition out of pocket so they might not even last two years."

"How you know?"

"It's common sense. Next thing you know they're back at home working at McDonald's, fighting child support, and telling their kids not to make the same mistakes they did. Do you want to end up like them?"

"Of course not."

"Then sit up front and pay attention. Oh, and you're welcome for your seat."

I had no choice but to do what she said; flipping burgers for a career wasn't exactly what I considered success. It just struck me how, in some small way, she actually seemed to care about me. I had forgotten what that felt like.

A few weeks had gone by and our conversation evolved discussing our views on politics, religion, and family. We hadn't discussed sex as much as I would have liked to, but in an effort to not be "that guy" I was going to wait for her to take the lead on that one. The lack of intimacy actually turned out to be a good thing. We always found a way to spend time together whether during lunch hours or after class. If there was a secluded place to go, we found it, and had those talks that made you late for everything else you had originally planned.

There was just one problem. The closer we got, the more I realized that she was way out of my league; the last time I checked, I wasn't ready for a relationship, and eventually I'd have to break the bad news. The *I'm just not ready for a relationship talk* was tricky because no matter how gently you tried to put it, you were going to end up being the bad guy and every nice thing you said and did was now a lie. But you meant the bad things, and they know next time to not ignore them. Same ole' same.

That "talk" usually happened after we had sex and after they tried to lock me down first. Danielle was in neither category, but she was either going to dislike me now or really hate me later, so it needed to happen immediately.

I ran her hypothetical responses, both physical and verbal, through my mind, Googled a couple of motivational quotes, then drove to her dorm where she'd be waiting for me to pick her up.

We had our nightly getaways by the city lake in my '99 Grand Am; that way we weren't in the privacy of my apartment and my car did more to turn girls off than on so it provided a safe ground for strictly non-physical interaction. We pulled up to our normal spot at the park, and while I still had my chest poked out, I went ahead and just spilled it.

"Danielle…there's something I've been meaning to tell you."

"Like what?"

"First, promise me you won't hate me."

"No. Now what is it?"

"So you gonna hate me?"

"Depending on what it is and especially if you keep beating around the bush. Now tell me. What is it?"

"All right. Well, here's the thing. I really like you. I think you're cool. I find you attractive and I enjoy kickin' it with you."

"Okay?"

"I'm just not ready to feel this way…yet. One day, I probably will but not right now. I got scars that need to heal, memories that need to be forgotten, and a bunch of other baggage you don't need. I can't settle down with you yet. I just can't."

"Hold on a second. I'm not asking you to settle down with me. I thought we were just getting to know each other."

"Yeah, we are…right now. But what happens when you fall in love with me? Then you're not going to want to leave me alone and it's going to be too late because you'll already be hooked."

"Shawn, is this one of your jokes?"

I shook my head. "No, I'm serious."

"Well, I think I can manage not getting 'hooked', but as for the rest, I'm not trying to push you into a relationship. I like you as much as you like me and I don't know what makes you say all this, but if you're not ready, then that's fine. *We* can't be ready until both of us are ready, and that's what matters."

"So you're not mad?"

"No, am I supposed to be?"

"I'm not saying that. I just figured you would-"

"Would be like all the other girls you told you wasn't ready for a relationship? Well, no, I'm not. As long as you can be honest with me about how you feel, take whatever time you need. I'm not going anywhere any time soon."

I felt her forehead to see if she had a fever. Nope. She was actually in her right mind.

I had gotten so used to dealing with dimes that a diamond was before me and I didn't know how to handle it. Guys like me weren't supposed to talk to girls like this.

I mean, in a perfect world, a relationship would be nice; a part of me was willing to go for it, but the rest of me remembers what it felt like the last time I did and branded serious relationships as something I needed to do when I was about 50, not 18. My last attempt at a relationship was back in high school but the lesson I learned from it was permanent: Life is a game that'll defeat anyone who refuses to play. I had developed quite a system to win, and so far it was working for me. But why does it seem like all the right people come at all the wrong times?

Game Over

For about the next month or so, Jazmin and I became distant. We texted often, but when I mentioned coming over just to speak, she stopped replying. I could do without overhearing her and Lewis knockin' the boots so coming over again unannounced was out of the question.

I was curious as to whether or not she told him the truth about who we used to be to each other, but I knew better. She was more adamant about forgetting that ever happened than I was. I never had feelings for Jazmin, but on some level I missed her presence. Sometimes you might not have an emotional connection with a person, but just having them around makes things better.

She was a rare breed, but the prototype for who I wanted in my circle. We could talk about anything and almost always were on the same page. She was like a homeboy put in a dream girl's body, and because there were no feelings involved, I didn't mind trusting her. My heart wasn't hers to break and her apathy for me gave me comfort.

At minimum, I wanted to see how my friend was doing and what she was up to. So, I started taking different routes to and from class, hoping that I'd just run into her, and got lucky one day. I caught her leaving class walking to her car.

"Hey yo, Jaz, what's up!? Where you been hiding girl?" I said, grinning, trying not to be so obvious about speeding up to cut her off from opening her car door.

"Well, hello, Mr. Shawn, I have been hiding in class. That's what we're in school for," she smirked. "How about you? You still cuttin' up, huh?"

"Actually no, I've been chilling. I don't even go out anymore unless it's with Danielle."

"That's the new girl, right? So she made it past two weeks? She must be special."

"Yeah, she really is. I don't wanna get my hopes up though. Anyway, how's what's-a-face treating you?"

"Lewis. And he's treating me great," she said, holding up her ring finger.

"Wow! A new promise ring. Nice."

"No, silly, it's an engagement ring. He asked me to marry 'em." she forced a smile and looked down.

"You sure sound excited."

"I mean I am. I guess it's just happening a little fast for me."

"When'd he propose?"

"Last month. We were celebrating his game-winning shot at Waffle House. He went over to the jukebox, put on a nice slow song, and then got on one knee. But I just bought the ring yesterday though."

"You bought what? Wait. Rewind. He proposed or did you?"

"He did, but he didn't have a ring. Said something about not wanting that to stop us and that he could always get it later, but I wanted to tell my fam, and there's no way I could do it without something on my finger. So, I went and bought it. He said he'll pay me back though."

"Well, congrats, I'm happy for you." Honestly, I didn't care. I was more relieved to have a reason behind her becoming distant. Her and her man were taking the next step; makes sense that he was getting more of her time and attention. I don't know how I feel about not being in the know exactly when this happened, but oh well. Good for her.

"If you want, we can double date," she said sarcastically. She knew better than to seriously invite me on a double date. Those are for couples who want to prove to their friends that everything they've been gossiping about is all true. Besides, I didn't want Danielle to get any ideas by me taking her out with a soon-to-be-married couple. That was a set-up.

"Nah, I'll pass, but make sure I get an invite to the wedding. When is that happening anyway, next week?"

"Ha ha, very funny. We haven't set a date yet. I think he's moving at a fast pace because he's more mature than most guys. Sometimes you gotta follow your heart and he understands that. Anyway, text me or something, I gotta go." She got in her car, checking her phone.

She probably thought nothing of it, but I felt like the advice she gave me was a sign. *Follow your heart*, she said. I don't know where it'll lead me, but it was worth a shot.

Things kept progressing between Danielle and me. Before class, I could always see her walking down the hall and how guys would try to get her attention. She'd either ignore or disrespect them without fail which always put a smile on my face. I couldn't blame them for trying; she was beautiful. But sometimes, I'd even go put my arm around her or some other public display of affection to rub it in. And when we got to the classroom, it didn't matter how many times I opened the door for her, she said thank you each and every time; unlike the other ungrateful ass females I opened the door for and they'd walk through without even making eye contact, as if it was owed to them. I wish I could trip them when they did that, but then I'd go to jail. Wasn't worth it.

But she appreciated the little things, especially when I told her about my childhood addiction to PB&J sandwiches and she decided to surprise me with two Ziploc bags, each with PB&J's in them; one had wheat bread and the other had white since I wasn't specific when I told her what I liked. That kind of stuff got to me. She was everything I never knew I always wanted.

Without a title, she was the only one I was seeing regularly and I completely neglected the friends-with-benefits chicks I had on my team. No regrets there. Hurting their feelings to keep the peace was a small price to pay. Besides, Danielle was teaching me how to do my own work so I didn't need them to *help me out* any more. Sex with girls you don't plan on having a future with is stressful. They're bound to want more; you're content on not giving it, and there's always that lingering 'Did the condom break?' afterthought.

I liked Danielle. A lot. My only concern was how scared of myself I was. What if I couldn't be the man she deserved right now? What if I waited too long and some other guy came and swept her off her feet?

I didn't want to get caught up in the moment and rush into anything, but the good ones don't wait around forever. Everyone knows that. She was making me a better person just by letting me know her, the type of girl you bring home to your parents, and she was tugging at my heart. Since that's what I was following, I was going to have to make her mine.

I'm a simple man, not too much of a romantic. If I had it my way, I would just go up to her, tell her I was ready to be together, and let her either agree or disagree. But I knew better.

So I tried to get creative. Go to the lake like we always did, and then out of nowhere recite a few lines I saw on a Hallmark card a while back. Girls love Hallmark cards, and besides, it's the thought that counts. I actually *thought* that would be a good idea.

We pulled up to the lake that night, cut the lights off, turned the slow jams down a bit, and reclined the seats.

"It's so nice out tonight, don't you think?" she said. "Just look at the stars. Don't they look nice?"

"Momma always told me, 'Never look directly into the light. It'll hurt your eyes', and I don't want my eyes to hurt."

"Shawn, stop it. If they were that bright it wouldn't be night time."

"Some of 'em so bright they keep shining after they're gone. Now that's a real star. Like Tupac."

She laughed. "That's funny. Sometimes I wonder what else is going on in that crazy head of yours."

"Actually, Danielle, there is this one thing. I've been wanting to say it and I guess now is as good a time as any."

"You don't have to say it. I already know."

"Hold up. What you mean you already know? How?"

"I saw you watching *Think Like A Man*. Don't worry, I don't have a 90-day rule. When the time is right, we'll know."

For a minute I thought she read my mind, but she was way off. I wasn't even thinking about sex. For once. Maybe I was changing after all. The old me had a 91-day rule anyway, and that was for girls who made me wait 90 days, I would be gone on the 91st. But even if she did have one, I would've stuck around. Maybe.

"Oh no, that's not it," I said, laughing. "No, what I'm tryna say is-" *my phone rang* "Uh..hold up real quick." I peeked at my phone and saw it was Jazmin. We had always texted, but now her ass wanted to chat.

It was going to have to wait. I tried to silence it without Danielle seeing the caller name on the screen.

"Hope it wasn't important."

I shifted in my seat. "Oh nah, just my homie. He probably ain't want nothin'," implicitly lying my ass off.

"But back to what I was saying. I…."My mind went blank. "Um.. Um. You see, I think, I mean I know. Well, I feel like..." I couldn't remember how that Hallmark card went to save my life.

"Danielle...I love you," I said. Straight to the point, unromantic as hell. I just came out with it.

She looked pleasantly stunned which turned quickly to suspicion. "Shawn, do you know what you're saying? If this is some kind of sick joke, it's not funny."

"No, it's not a joke, and yes, I do know what I'm saying. More importantly, I know what I'm feeling. I'm in love with you. It's not enough to just *kinda* have you anymore. I want all of you and I want to give you all of me. If you'll have me, I want you to be my girlfriend." My heart was beating faster than Usain Bolt on crack. Every second she took to make some kind of reaction seemed like an hour. So of course, she sat there and let it all soak in before she finally spoke.

"Wow. I didn't see that coming. Well, I love you too. I knew you were unsure about whether or not you could do the relationship thing so I wasn't going to pressure you. And-"

"But you didn't pressure me."

"Shawn, can I speak please?" I caught myself and waited for her to talk again.

"Like I was saying, I just didn't know if you felt ready for the responsibility of my heart. But I believe in you. You're a great guy and I don't think you even realize it. So yes, I'd love to be your girl."

I tried to hold back my smile, and failed. She believed in me. That's music to any man's ears. So there it was. I was officially off the market. I was taken.

The Calm Before the Storm

I made the transition into being a boyfriend better than I thought I would. There were girls I saw everyday that I'd previously flirted with, and now I acted like I'd never met them. They caught attitudes about it, but a sacrifice had to be made, and I was happy to make it. Had to block a few of them on Facebook because spiteful females can get creative with old pic messages and text message screenshots. Things nobody could really explain.

Meanwhile, Danielle and I were damn near joined at the hip, ankle, and shoulder everywhere we went. You know the couple you see walking in the mall with their hands in each other's back pocket, and their steps are synchronized? Yeah, that was us. You could've sprayed us with a water hose and it still wouldn't have rained on our parade.

She was my beautiful best friend.

Things were lovely, but the summer break was already approaching. Three months in, she was going back to her hometown in Denver, Colorado, and I was staying in Alabama. Bitter-sweet because I wasn't ready to leave her, but it was due time to see my family too.

I hadn't made any plans for my summer outside of staying in shape to come back ready for the football season. Wasn't too hopeful on finding a job since employers weren't looking for overqualified seasonal workers with a high school diploma. I was cool with that because being overworked and underappreciated leads to stress. Stress leads to cancer. Nobody wants cancer.

Momma and Mr. Macklin were still going strong and had been enjoying having the house to themselves. I could tell by how half-heartedly they welcomed me back. I saw them peeking out the window when I pulled up in the driveway, both of them, just watching in despondency. But they at least had the decency to put on a smile and pretend they were happy. The effort was there and I appreciated it.

The house was lonely compared to my days in high school. All of my stuff had been cleaned out of my old room and Alvin's old room was the new storage. He dropped out of college after his first semester and went to live with his girlfriend, so while the parent's were at work, it was just me by my lonesome.

That turned out to be a good thing because it got awkward when Mr. Macklin came around. He was skeptical about everything, particularly a college he was successful without.

One day he came home from work and saw me in the kitchen. I was putting up the dishes and he sat there staring at me. I stared back until he got his thoughts together.

Then he said, "Oh, so you a college boy now. You know everythang, huh? Well, tell me this. How come they don't put real lemons in lemonade, but they put real lemons in lemon-fresh Pine Sol?"

He had a million of these *you're not so smart after all* comments in his back pocket. Probably derivative of his disappointment in his own jr.

"The same reason that real lemons are in Pine Sol, but if you drink it, you'll die. Lemons aren't good for you," I said, walking off like a boss.

I made no more sense than did his trivial ass question and purposely so.

After getting used to having my freedom, I was ill-adjusting to having a curfew. Momma was irritable seemingly every day, and going in and out of the house late at night was like asking her to remind me who paid the bills.

About halfway through the break, I was ready to go back. I was horny and hungry 24/7 since Danielle wasn't there, and Momma refused to cook. My old friends from high school were either out of town or already suffering from the real world. The ones that never left had started families, worked multiple 9-5's, and some had gotten caught up in the system.

The tension in the house had gotten thick. Momma and Mr. Macklin were hardly talking and a few times I even noticed him sleeping on the couch.

I tried to find little odd jobs to keep me busy and pretend I didn't notice what was happening but I know they knew. They would take it out on me with pointless arguments about things not being picked up around the house, so I started leaving in the mornings and coming back around curfew.

The summer was coming to an end, and so was I on my rope. I just had to get my expenses straightened out before pre-registration started so I could go back to camp in a few weeks.

My books were the only things not covered by my athletic scholarship, and I needed them to even get into class. I had made a little money, but it was only enough for extracurricular activities. That was the agreement I had since I started working at 15. I made enough to buy what I wanted and Momma would provide the things I needed so long as I stayed out of trouble. But Momma was no longer the breadwinner. Mr. Macklin was.

I hated asking for things and especially from Mr. Macklin because I could count on him giving a smart ass response, but I didn't have a choice. I was going to have to swallow my pride.

It was July 17th, only three days before my birthday, so I thought maybe this'd make the gift choosing a little easier anyway.

He came home from work and I heard him go straight to his room as usual. I went and knocked on his door.

"Who is it?" he said.

"It's me."

"Come in."

I guess that was his way of showing me he wore the big pants. He knew good and well it was me, but authority over even the small things made him feel more in charge.

"Hey Mr. Macklin, can I ask you something?"

"Ya just did. So yeah, now is that all?"

"No, not that question. I got another question."

"If it's 'bout money, I ain't got it."

"No, it's about school...books. I need money to get them."

"How come you can't pay for 'em?"

"Well, I didn't make that much this summer, and what I did make, I already spent."

"A man's 'posed to make the money he need to get what he need. You a man now, that's yo responsibility. Find a way to get the money."

"If I'm such a man then why you claiming me on your taxes?" I never took this tone with him before, but I couldn't believe he pulled the whole *man card* on me for asking for a necessary school expense. School that he bragged about to his church family but didn't have to pay a dime for tuition out-of-pocket. This was the least he could do.

He shifted and said, "Boy, you watch yo tone. You still in my house."

He was right. Whether he was my real dad or if I agreed with him or not, he provided the roof and any rules up under it had to be respected.

"All right then, my bad."

"You can't come in here just demanding stuff 'cuz you needs it."

"I know that's my bad. I shouldn't have said that."

"I didn't have nothin' growin up. Not no car. Not no college. Nothin'. I got out here and worked for everythang with my bare hands."

"I got it, Mr. Macklin. I said that was my bad. I'm sorry. My bad for asking you for help even though I really do need it," I said, turning and walking out.

I hated hearing no, especially from a man. It just felt like a slap in the face for some reason.

Either way, I wasn't stressing. I knew enough people that I could borrow books from to get me through the first part of the semester.

Mr. Macklin was a pretty cool dude until he got into one of his moods. He must have been in one of them that day because when Momma got home, they started fussing. I guess that's what happens when you get in a marriage at such a mature age. You're stuck in your ways so arguments become the protocol to remain stuck in them.

It was late. Instead of eavesdropping, I opted for some much-needed rest. The more sleep, the faster the days went by.

A couple of hours later, I was awakened by some thumping noises and yelling. I took a glance at the alarm clock and saw it was 3:15 a.m. Nothing should've been more important than sleep at that hour.

"I'm tired of this shit! You and him both can get the hell out my house!" I heard coming from across the hallway.

My door flung open. Mr. Macklin was sweating and had an evil look in his eye. This wasn't the country, soul music-loving man I had come to know.

"You wanna be a man, then be a man and help yo Momma get her shit packed," he said before he walked back into his room.

I lit up with anger. What in the hell got into him? He had to be drunk or something. I could have put my hands on him but I was more concerned about Momma. I had to make sure she was okay because if she wasn't, I wouldn't leave a single wall standing in that house.

My mind was alert but my body was still waking up. Trying not to stumble I slipped on a shirt and gym shoes and rushed out into the living room to find Momma on the floor crying.

"Momma, you all right? Did he hit you?"

She shook her head no, still crying. I felt relieved, but we still needed to get our things together and get out. No way were we about to stay where we weren't welcomed.

Mr. Macklin came back in the living room with his arms full of Momma's clothes.

"The hell y'all waitin' on? I said get out!" he yelled, tossing her things on the ground.

I had enough of his shit. "Man, what's your problem?!"

He looked at me, still breathing heavy. "You. You my problem. You come 'round here like you better than err'body then got the nerve to ask me for somethin'? Cuz you in college now, you 'posed to be somebody? Well, you ain't. You ain't nobody and you ain't gon' be

70

nobody. AND you gon' get the hell out my house and take ya momma witcha."

"You know what bruh, fuck you. We ain't gotta take this."

"Baby, just…just go." I turned around and saw Momma looking at me.

"Wait….what?"

"Just go. You need to get out of here." she said again.

I had never been shot before, but if I had to guess what it felt like, it was about half as painful as what I felt then.

"Momma no. You don't know what you saying. I'mma help you get your stuff and we can just-"

"No son. You need to go. The longer you stay the worse this is going to get."

I looked at Mr. Macklin, then back at Momma. Mr. Macklin walked back into his room. Momma looked down at the floor, avoiding eye contact.

I backed up a few steps and stood paralyzed from the neck up. I couldn't blink; I couldn't breathe; I could only hear my heart beating.

Mr. Macklin was one thing, but there's no way she was choosing him over me. I wasn't completely sure of what was going on, but I needed to act then and finish thinking later. I went to the room, grabbed my duffle bag, and crammed what I could into it. Walked out into the living room and saw Mr. Macklin and Momma sitting on the couch.

"One day, you gon' look back and realize I was right about you." he said as I opened the door. I pretended to not hear him and kept walking but those words all but missed my ears.

I started up the Grand Am and pulled off. At first I didn't have a destination; I just needed to get away. I could go to my sister's house, but that'd require an explanation and I really didn't feel like talking. Since football camp was a few weeks away, I decided to just drive the two hours back to campus and find a place to lay my head.

I ran every red light through downtown to the highway. Luckily, it was about four in the morning so there wasn't any traffic. My thoughts were skipping worse than an old CD player.

Did my mother just side with this man she met 4 years ago over me? My world was flipped upside down. Memories of my childhood of me in kindergarten, going to my first day in school, and times I gave her homemade birthday cards began sending piercing pains through my chest. Those times alone should've been enough for her to have my back.

And then I thought about his words, *You gone look back and realize I was right about you.* For the first time in my life, I hated someone. I glanced down at the dashboard and caught myself going 120 miles per hour in a car that was in desperate need of new tires, so I slowed down. The I-85 north was dark and monotonous, forcing me to focus on everything I didn't want to realize.

I thought to myself, *So this is what it feels like to be an orphan.* Because that's how it seemed. Over dramatic? Maybe. But it hurt like hell. I cried, then I sucked it up, then I cried again. I needed somebody to come and explain to me what the hell was going on. I wanted to throw up. I wanted to give up. But I just kept driving.

I finally made it back near campus and my gas light reminded me of another grim reality. I was broke. Usually, I could squeeze about 20 more miles after the gas hand hit zero and I was close to campus, so I went ahead and pulled into a Wal-Mart parking lot nearby. If I needed a bathroom or other daily amenities, this was about as close to the Hilton as I'd get.

After three hours of sleep and one hell of an emotional night, I was exhausted. I took some sweats out my duffle bag, folded them up, and used them as a pillow. Let the seat all the way back and took the key out the ignition. The sun was on its way up, but broad daylight was no match for how much I needed to close my eyes and mentally exhale.

I woke up a few hours later, checked my phone, saw three missed calls from Danielle. We always started the day off with my good morning text, a reply if she beat me to it, so she had to know something was up. My pride was telling me to keep this to myself; nobody needed to know I was put out on my ass and basically disowned by my mother.

I texted her back.

Sorry I missed your text. That was some good sleep. Lol.

She replied,

Oh well, that's good you got some rest. I didn't. I had a bad dream something happened to you. Can you talk?

Well, so much for getting out of that one. I never believed in dreams being like premonitions, but this was quite the coincidence. Before I could find her number in my contacts, I got her incoming call.

"Hello?"

"Hey, Superman. You busy?" Superman was her pet name she picked out for me one night we were cuddling. I picked her out one too, but I realized how Twilight-ish it sounded so I rarely used it.

"Nah, just at Wal- Mart picking up a few things. What's going on?"

"I just wanted to call. You sound like something's wrong. You okay?"

Damn am I that obvious? I thought. I was holding it together pretty well all things considered. This was my girl though. If there was anybody I could go to, it was her. I didn't like lying to her, and she'd eventually find out anyway.

"Yeah, I am. Okay…no, I'm not," I admitted.

"What happened?"

"A lot. Last night Mr. Macklin and Momma got into it and they kicked me out."

"Hold on, why did they kick you out? What did you have to do with it?"

"I'm not really sure, I think it had something to do with me asking Mr. Macklin for books or something. I don't know. All I know is, in the middle of the night I got woke up and 20 minutes later I was packing my things." I looked outside to make sure no one was watching. Parking lots are good for making a person paranoid.

"What about your mom? She didn't stop him?"

"No, she helped him. He was kicking us both out but then she… Look I don't wanna talk about this right now. I got a lot on my mind."

"Then she what?"

"I said I don't wanna talk about it."

"Okay, I'm sorry. Where are you?"

"I told you, I'm at Wal-Mart. That's where I'm staying until I can get in touch with somebody."

"Superman, you can't stay there. It's dangerous and you need to eat. I'm going to send you some money."

"No, don't do that."

"Why? You need to eat."

"Just…don't. I gotta figure this out on my own." The last thing I needed was another hand out. My pride was shot, I was still angry, but too fragile to trust someone's help.

"Superman, let me help you. It's really not a problem. I'll just give you enough to last you until you get a place to stay," she said. I don't care how much money she had, my pride was about all that was keeping me going, and I couldn't abandon that now.

"I said no. I'll talk to you later. I gotta go." I hung up.

I didn't want anybody else giving me something they could take away. Not money, things, or even love. If I didn't already have it, I must not need it.

Looking in my glove compartment, I found $20 I had stashed away for emergencies. I had another $7 in my wallet, and $1.75 in quarters that had dropped in between the seats. If I budgeted just right, I knew I could stretch it over the next two weeks and make it to football camp where they'd serve food then. Hell, I didn't have a choice.

I dug in my duffle bag and grabbed my toothbrush and wash cloth, then walked into Wal-Mart. It wasn't overly crowded, just a few elderly shoppers having their weekly thrill of pushing around the shopping buggy before the working world got off.

It was mid afternoon and I still had morning breath, so I immediately went over to the cosmetics section and snatched up some toothpaste. I had never stolen anything, but I feel like God was giving me a pass on this one. Besides, He told me to treat others how I wanted to be treated, and I'd hate it if anyone gathered the audacity to talk to me with breath like mine.

I went to the bathroom and killed my dragon. I didn't have the luxury of a shower, so a toilet stall would have to do. I wet my rag, put some hand soap in it, and scrubbed the hot spots(armpits and genitals). When the coast was clear, I ran out, rinsed the rag, and wiped one more time. That was the hygiene routine from then on.

Still hungry and needing to pinch every penny possible, I started plotting on the produce section. The plums never looked so juicy and the apples were practically taunting me. I grabbed a stranded cart nearby to pretend I was casually shopping, then loaded a few in.

The camping section toward the very back was always empty so I knew I could count on enough privacy for a quick meal there.

Casually, I walked through the store whistling and pretending to browse along the way, and when I got to the back, I ate the fruit like table-manners were my nemesis.

They were sweeter than candy, hitting all the right spots to my aching stomach. When I was done, I neatly stashed the seeds behind a tent that was on display. You know, out of courtesy.

I walked back outside and sat in the car; of course, the sun would be at full strength. It was a little too much to ask that a cloud find its way between us, but I wasn't complaining. It beat sitting under a bridge any day.

A few days went by and the employees were starting to recognize me. I could tell by the stares and cutting eyes when I walked in. I had to change up my sleeping pattern so I could go in during different shifts. Made sure I changed clothes and moved my car to different areas to throw any suspicious minds off from realizing I had set up camp at Wal-Mart.

I didn't get out of the car much. The last thing I needed was anybody from school to recognize me and put me on blast for being a car roof away from homeless.

On the bright side, it gave me time to dwell a bit and mentally organize myself.

Danielle was growing increasingly worried about me, and Momma had even called a few times. Probably trying to wish me a happy birthday. I refused to answer. There was no way I could bring myself to hear her voice after what it meant the last time I did.

A part of me wondered what happened the rest of the night between them and the other part of me was still hurting from the fact she didn't come to my defense whether they had decided I was wrong or not. That was my momma. I was her son. I wasn't the only one she had, but she was the only one I had. She was supposed to be there for me.

Feeling alone was becoming less and less a strange feeling and I began reconsidering what I thought I knew about love. It's misleadingly great because the more of it you have the more there is to lose. And when you lose it, it hurts like hell.

I could see why Eminem bashed his mother. Not because he's hateful, but because he believed in a love he at some point realized he didn't have. I wasn't able to go as far as bashing mine, but I could relate.

Jazmin and I spoke every other week or so and this wasn't that week. I woke up and didn't see Danielle's good morning wishes, so I went ahead and texted her first. She was the only person I was communicating with since I had gotten kicked out.

I went inside and cleaned myself up, got some more fruits and vegetables, and came back to lie in the car. I still didn't see a text reply. It wasn't like her to not hit me back, especially with what had happened. I wasn't about to stress it though.

Since I never quite got a full night's rest in the driver's seat, I could always go for another nap anyway. As soon as I began dozing off I heard an engine pull up in the parking spot next to mine. I was in the far side of the lot and had managed to stay out of sight thus far, so I started getting nervous.

I guess I couldn't expect to hide forever. In Alabama, the police were looking for a reason to harass a black man who looked like he was down on his luck.

I returned the seat to full position so I could see who it was, and Danielle was standing outside my window.

"Well, are you gonna just sit there and stare or are you going to let me in?" she said, smiling from ear to ear.

I smiled back, doing so for the first time in a week. I was so surprised, my words were all fighting to get out at once and couldn't. There was a rush of energy flowing back to me; my heartbeat sped up, and I had forgotten all about my scruffy appearance. I found the unlock button and pressed it to let her in. She jumped in and all but broke my neck hugging me.

"Supermaaaan!!!!" she yelled. "I missed you so much. Are you okay?" she said, using the same outside voice she used before.

"Yeah, I'm fine. When did you get here? Why didn't you tell me you were-"

"I just got here a few hours ago and came straight from the airport. You said you were at Wal-Mart and this is the closest one to school. I knew if I told you I was coming, you'd just talk me out of it so....I didn't."

Interesting. Maybe God was showing me he hadn't forgotten about me. I always believed He placed people in my life for a reason, and hers was all too clear to me at that moment. She was my partner, and partners always have each other's back.

"Well, it's good to see you. I missed you so much. You really didn't have to fly all the way down here though, Danielle."

"I know I didn't, but I wasn't about to let you stay in this dirty parking lot. I got a hotel room for us up the street and we still need to celebrate your birthday. We can go there so you can-"

"No."

She cocked her head to one side. "No what?"

"I'm not going to a hotel. I'll be fine here until football camp starts, only a few more days anyway."

"Superman, why won't you let me help you?"

"Because I can't go through life depending on people. It's time for me to grow up and be a man. Stand on my own two. I'll be fine right here." My pride was butting in.

"Well, I'm staying here with you then," she said as she leaned over and put her head on my chest. "If you don't wanna stay in a hotel, then I don't wanna stay in one either."

I didn't know if she was calling my bluff or what, but something about that touched me. There was no way I could let her sleep in a car, though, not on my account. If she was going to be that stubborn then I would just have to give in and go to the hotel. I put the key in the ignition and started the car.

She raised her head and looked at me. "Where are you going?"

"*We* are going to the hotel. No need in wasting a perfectly good room." Just the feeling of her lying on my chest had my hormones waking up and stretching from the nap they took in her absence. She looked back at me and smiled.

The Good, The Bad, and The I'll Open My Eyes When It's Over

Going back to school was a completely different experience. Never before had I been so motivated to prove someone wrong with the level of determination I had this time. While I was fueled by negative experiences, the outcome was positive.

I was focused more in the classroom, doing my own work and seeing my professors in their offices to debate the chapters. My football stats went through the roof and I was becoming a household name on campus for the plays I made. I had even begun reconciling my differences with Momma after pressure from my sisters, but knowing her husband on any level was a thing of the past. Mr. Macklin was as good as dead to me. My only ray of sanity left was in my relationship with God and Danielle and I had no problem with that. I had a newfound appreciation for her and what she brought to the table.

I was so in love that I never felt like I was doing enough to give her the same euphoric feeling she gave me. It kept me on my P's and Q's, always trying to make her smile harder than the time before.

I explored loving her more creatively by surprising her with celebrations of anniversaries as simple as the first time we held hands, just to give me a reason to cater to her. Most of those celebrations consisted of overnight bubble baths, massages, and passionate sex, sometimes playful teasing with different edibles, other times poems I would write and memorize to recite in front of her friends to her. And she ate it up every single time.

I loved her deeper mentally and emotionally. I set aside time uninterrupted by any other obligation just to listen to and understand her more. I made it a habit to let her vent about her day while I rubbed her feet and greased her scalp. Sometimes, it bored the shit out of me, but I managed to find questions to keep her talking so she could feel like I was interested.

When she got off late from her part-time job at Sonic, I came and sat in the parking lot until she came out so I could escort her home safely. I was willing to protect her by any means necessary, and somewhat even anxious for a chance to.

I was still *college student* broke. Scraping pennies was the norm and I'd be damned if I ever walked past a nickel I saw lying on the ground. But she didn't mind. Most females wouldn't give the time of day to a brother with no job regardless of his potential, but she never made it an issue. Top Ramen noodles with hotdog slices, strong wifi signal, a Netflix movie, and we were good to go for an evening full of quality time that beat going to any five-star restaurant out there.

Going into the second year of our relationship, we decided to move in together to keep from paying two sets of bills when all we did was sleep over at the other's place anyway. We wanted to make it as close to a traditional household as possible, so I agreed to pay the bills with my school refund check, and she could handle the groceries and furniture.

I couldn't wait till the day when I could just tell her, "Baby don't worry, I got this. Keep your money and go buy yourself something nice," but in the interest of reality, I just didn't have it like that. Splitting the bills would also free up a little space in my budget to start saving for a ring.

I had finally gotten to a point where I was ready to settle down and get married. I wanted the wedding, I wanted a small house we could renovate together with occasional quickies, I wanted to pick out baby names and argue about who's features would make the cutest baby. I wanted it all. It just seemed right. Well, everything except the money. But I figured if I started saving early, maybe I could have a decent down payment for a ring by the time we graduated two years later. Oh, and I would have to earn her mother's blessing...somehow.

We less than hit it off the first time I talked to her. Not sure if it was something I said, but eventually, I figured she'd come around. She'd see, just like the rest of the world, my love for her daughter was real and undeniable. That's what any parent should want for their child.

Jazmin and I still kept in touch via Facebook and text message, but I had not seen her for months now. From the pictures, she looked happy and equally in love as I was. A part of me missed the emotionally-detached conversation I could have with a girl who wanted nothing from me, but neither of our situations were going to facilitate that friendship any longer.

I had yet to introduce her to Danielle, but I didn't see much of a purpose since we were barely even on "Hey, how you been?" terms. Danielle would want to know of any friendship I had with a girl, but telling her about this one and at this point was only going to raise unnecessary eyebrows that I could do without. It bothered me because I had to try to erase my tracks the few times I did message or text Jazmin, something I hated making a habit of. I didn't realize just how much of a mistake this would turn out to be.

Danielle met some new friends at her job who were all too curious about what exactly it was that kept her so happily in love with me and what she did to get me whipped. I didn't mind at first, it even made me proud to give her something to brag about. But spectators belong in the stands, not on the court. Or else there's chaos and everyone loses.

Since Danielle didn't have much of a past love-life to compare ours to, I was insecure about how sure she was that what we had was exactly what she wanted. Just my luck, her friends had all been scorned by guys, turning them into hostile feminists who began filling her head with their own experiences that warranted a further check into my extra-curricular social engagements. There was no way that all of them had these ain't-shit guys and she just so happened to stumble upon 'Mr. Right' on her very first try. No way, so they felt.

It wasn't long before she started asking questions like "So why is it that you *really* love me?" and "Out of all the girls, why me?" To some extent, one can expect his woman to ask these questions just for re-affirmation, but I knew exactly the source. There was a hot topic in her circle of friends and it was revolving around me.

"Baby, I love you because of who you are. You're dedicated to us as a team, and you're a perfect fit for what I'm striving to become."

She seemed pleased with my reply but only briefly. "Well, what kind of fit am I for who you are right now?"

"You're a great fit, Danielle. Wait, where is all this coming from anyway?"

"Just asking," she said dismissively.

It worked my nerves when she did this but I knew that no relationship was perfect. Everyone has somebody who can push their buttons.

I came out of the shower one night to see her glaring at me.

"So…when were you going to tell me about Jazmin?" she growled.

I was caught off guard. So I said what most guys' first response is when we need a second to think. "Who?"

"Jazmin. I heard y'all go way back."

"Oh... *Jazmin* Jazmin. She's an old friend of mine. Who told you this?"

"Don't worry about it. You should've been the one telling me. You tryna hide something? What is it you need to tell me?" I hated how women never reveal who they're getting their inside information from because they didn't want it to stop.

"Look, me and Jazmin used to kick it way before you, that's it. Nothing more than that I promise. I haven't even seen her in months."

"So why she still texting you then and at almost 11 o'clock at night?"

"Wait, you going through my phone now?" I said, getting a temper of my own. I don't care what it was she found or didn't find, going through my phone was a violation of trust. She had no right.

"I didn't go through anything. It was lying face up when she texted you. Make sure you respond. We don't like when guys take too long to respond, ya know," She said, turning over in the covers.

I wanted to explain the situation in full, but I was a little pissed off that my trust had been violated. We had a relationship where it was always a priority, and even though she didn't cross any lines, I kept my phone unlocked for that reason. But if the tables were turned, I would've probably done the same thing, so I let it go.

We were going to have to discuss this sooner or later, but now wasn't the time. I slid under the covers beside her, kissed her cheek, and whispered "I'm sorry and I love you." She didn't respond. I guess she was more upset than I thought.

Out of curiosity, I checked the text from Jazmin to see what it said. It was odd for her to be texting me so late at night, especially now that she had a man. I looked and saw that it was a mass text message invite to her engagement party. I wished she was a little more thoughtful about who was in that contact list.

I called her first thing in the morning. Now her existence and our history was out in the open, there needed to be some rules of my own in place. I waited until Danielle was gone to her first class to call, only for it to go straight to voicemail.

"Hey, sorry I couldn't get to my phone. Leave a message and I'll get back with you shortly."

Beep

"Hey, Jaz, this is Shawn. I wanted to talk to you when you got the chance so when you can, please, give me a call. Thanks."

Great. I just told her to call me back at no definite time of when to do so. And on top of that, I was paranoid about what else Danielle could possibly "hear". Fortunately, there was some truth to this news, but what if there wasn't in the future?

She used to be pretty good about not paying attention to rumors, but a new female friend she knew nothing about before could definitely open the door to more assumptions. I needed to stop being so careless and lock my phone like other guys. Whether or not you have anything to hide, perception is still reality.

After that night, our relationship was no longer in the honey moon phase. We began having real problems. She was wanting me to open up more and talk, and I was battling the influence of her *"friends"* who were teaching her how to not trust me all of a sudden. Me against all of them wasn't a fair fight. Some "friends" will make you feel like what you have is too good to be true because they never had it.

I never got a return call from Jazmin but that might've been a good thing considering her timing. I was more focused on settling the real issue, and that was strictly between Danielle and me. No matter what it was, I was confident we could work through it. Every relationship comes with its ups and downs and I was along for the ride.

As the months went on, Danielle's behavior became more and more strange. She got closer to her friends and more distant from me. We went from having sex twice a day to twice a week to not at all for a month straight. Every time I brought it up, she just gave me an excuse about how she wasn't feeling well.

I thought maybe she was pregnant, but I knew her menstrual cycle like clockwork, and she hadn't missed a beat. The meals she cooked became less frequent until it was just me cooking and when I did cook for both of us, she wasn't hungry.

Her demeanor completely changed. A girl from the suburbs who never set foot in a club before was all of a sudden staying out all night without so much as a call to say she wouldn't be back. That kept me up worried sick, driving around town to see if I could find her, not because I was jealous, but because I never could sleep without knowing that she was safe. A few drinks turned into being too intoxicated to drive home, and I struggled to explain why it rubbed me the wrong way that she was acting like...like a normal college girl. But I knew it didn't feel right.

We were spiraling out of control and an end to our relationship seemed inevitable. I felt helpless, like I was getting jacked in an alleyway by thugs, two holding my arms and the other taking his best shot at my stomach. I simply did not know what to do, but I did know that giving up wasn't an option.

With anything in life, it's easy to stray away from the basics, so I figured maybe that's where I went wrong. Maybe she felt like I didn't care, or wasn't giving her the same attention as before. With all the stress of going to school, trying to work, and maintain as a couple, I'm sure it would get tough on anyone.

I decided to take a few steps back, check the man in the mirror, and remind her of why she chose me in the first place. I still had a few tricks up my sleeve, and this was as good a time as any to pull them out. Operation "Remind(h)er" was in full effect.

She had Saturdays off, so I waited until Friday and pulled every dime out of my savings account that I had saved up for the ring. Hell, if this didn't work I wouldn't need it anyway. I took the money and went and got pictures we took in the earlier stages of our relationship printed and framed to hang around the house. This was going to be the visual reminder.

I made a mixed CD of the songs we listened to on the way to and from our first date. I remember the feeling when I first made the playlist and how I carefully picked each song to take us through our conversation. A little upbeat at the beginning to loosen things up, neo soul in the middle for stimulating talks, and some throwback 90's jams to make sure I stayed on her mind. This would be the auditory reminder.

Lastly, I bought two gallons of milk, rose petals, and candles. Soaking in a milk bath under rose petals with candles all around should set the tone for some quality interaction. I didn't know much about wine other than the fact that women love it, and that it was made from spoiled grapes, but I got some of that too. A little alcohol in her system with some pampering should loosen her up just right for me to put in work later on in the evening. This would be the physical reminder.

She usually went straight from class to work until about 10 p.m. which played perfectly into my plan. It gave me time to get a haircut and have the place cleaned up. I scrubbed everything from top to bottom, washed and folded every piece of clothing, and even set out some potpourri.

With about an hour left before she would get home, I heated the milk on the stove-top and ran the bath water. After the tub was half full, I poured the steaming hot milk into the tub and spread the rose petals on top of it. Carefully, I placed the candles on the sink and toilet top to set the ambiance just right.

It was about 10 minutes until she would be pulling up and I felt myself getting anxious. Catering to her was nothing new for me, but I still reached behind me and patted myself on the back. I had the house looking like something from a Zane novel.

I got the wine out of the freezer and set it by the tub with two wine glasses. I heard her engine pulling up then cutting off in the driveway. I ran around the house cutting the lights off, pressed play on the stereo and unlocked the door for her, leaving it cracked.

She walked in looking confused. "Superman....?"

"Hey, baby, how was your day?" I said daring her to actually tell me about her day instead of commenting on the environmental masterpiece I had created.

"What is all of this? It's not our anniversary or my birthday.," she said walking in slowly looking around at the pictures.

I took her jacket for her and gently came up from behind wrapping my arms around her waist. "I know, I just felt like we needed to talk about some things and I want to make you as comfortable as possible in the process. You like it?"

"I love it. It's beautiful. I mean really, it's amazing, I can't believe you would do all this for me."

"I know, I know. But that's 'cause you worth it and I got even more planned for us tonight. Got a little wine, got a little bath water, got a little-"

"But I'm really tired and I had a long day. I hate to rain on your parade because I appreciate all this. I do. But I'm just beat, and I need some rest. Maybe we can do it tomorrow."

Surely, she didn't seriously think I was going to re-do all of this *tomorrow*. "I know you're tired. That's why all I want you to do is get undressed out your clothes and relax a bit. I'll do everything else."

"Superman, this is all really nice. Really, it is. But I had two exams. We were slammed at work all day, I really just want to get my shower and get in bed."

That was the straw that broke the black camel's back. I went over and pressed pause on the music so she could hear every word I had to say. "How come you don't just at least try to enjoy this? I put a lot of work into getting everything set up for you and all you can talk about is sleep? What is it with you?"

"What is it with me? I just got home from work and I'm tired, and I'm going to sleep. You don't think about anybody but your damn self. You don't like it? Get over it or get out," she said, her voice raised much higher than usual.

"Wait, this is my house too. What you mean get out? I pay bills in here just like you do."

"Oh please. If it wasn't for me you would still be sleeping in Wal-Mart parking lots."

That struck a nerve. A very large one at that. "Danielle...what did you just say to me?"

"I said, if it wasn't for me you wouldn't have shit. You think because you pay a few bills that you in charge, but you're not. I let you pay these bills so you can feel good about yourself, but I don't need you for anything. I can pay all this on my own. Matter of fact, this is my house more than it is yours."

That was it. Memories of being in that parking lot were still fresh wounds, and those words poured salt all over them. I knew she was acting strange, but this was a completely different person.

The worst part about it was, I let it be true. I promised myself not to let anyone give me a rug they'd eventually snatch from under my feet. I broke that promise to myself for her.

The embarrassment of that reality, the frustration that the plans I had for the night were going up in flames, on top of everything else leading up to that point just sent my anger to an unsafe level. Staying there wasn't going to be good for either one of us.

"I can't...I can't believe you just said that to me."

She looked down as if she was just now realizing the weight of her words. "All I'm saying is-"

"Fuck your money, fuck everything you bought me, *and* fuck you." I put on my shoes, grabbed my keys, and left. Got in my car and slammed the door shut. I needed something to help me forget what just happened.

My mind was racing. I needed help. Why she would stoop so low to hurt me and where this was coming from were questions I couldn't answer soon enough.

After a few hours of driving around, I came back to the house to see that her car was gone. Normally I'd be curious as to where or if she was okay but this time I didn't care. I was still upset from the word exchange earlier, and it all *but* went away when I came back inside.

The entire house had been cleaned out with the exception of the furniture and the clothing I originally brought to school with me the summer before. The bed sheets, the comforter, the microwave, the TV, my clothes, even my toothbrush. Gone.

I don't know if this was a test, but in my mind, we were over, completely. This is the kind of thing people do when they're trying to break you. People only try to break you when they hate you, but I did nothing to deserve her hate.

I felt like I had just gotten woken up from a weird dream. I had that moment when you yawn and realize that everything you thought was real was only in your imagination.

I flopped down on the naked mattress to let things soak in a bit and ended up dozing off. Sleep was about the only thing I had to look forward to.

I woke up the next morning and checked my Facebook to see her indirectly insulting the hell out of me. She had went on an all-out *I need a real* man status update rant with her closest friends all cosigning and *liking* every status.

A few of them read:

"A real man knows a real woman when he sees her. But some guys seem to be blind."

"Disliking me is okay. Disagreeing is fine too. But disrespect me and you will be dismissed."

"I give you two chances to earn my trust. 3 strikes is for games, and I don't play those."

Annoyed, I slammed my laptop closed and went to get something to eat just to find that she took the food too. Spiteful. I was the kind of hungry that you get when you want something so bad, you don't have the energy to make it yourself.

To think, all this started back when she saw the text from Jazmin. That and her friends giving the back story on our friendship. While I was thinking of her, I decided to hit her up. My stomach was on E, and her cooking never disappointed.

The last I heard, she was still planning on marrying Lewis, but that shouldn't stop her from giving me her extras should she have any from breakfast she surely made that morning. I sent her a text to let her know I was on my way. Maybe she'd be willing to listen to my soap opera while she was at it.

I got over to her apartment, and to my pleasant surprise I could smell a sausage and eggs aroma seeping through the door. It didn't matter how bad of a day I was having, the smell of breakfast always put a smile on my heart. I opened the door and saw Jazmin in her Victoria's Secret black-laced boy shorts and matching bra in front of the stove.

"Damn, Jaz, you tryna seduce me?" I said, walking in. I hadn't seen a girl cooking in underwear since the morning after Danielle and I broke in the new apartment. I was still upset over the fight but my hormones had shaken it off.

She snapped around. "Shawn, what the hell?! What are you doing here?!" she yelled running back into the room.

"Well, I texted you. I was tryna see if you were cooking, and now I'm tryna see if you're sharing."

She came back out with a t-shirt on, as if they made her 'decent' for company. "Oh I didn't see it. But yeah you can have some. What happened? Danielle didn't cook?"

"About that, yeah, I don't know if we're even together anymore."

"Oh no! What did you do?!"

"Before we get to that, is Lewis here?"

"No."

"Okay good, cuz I don't want no shit. But umm, I didn't do anything. It's a long story, but basically, we've been having problems for a while now. I tried to talk it out last night and it turned into a big argument. We said some things that shouldn't have been said; she moved out; I'm here. I'm hungry."

"Yeah, I was wondering what was going on when I saw her statuses on Facebook."

If Jazmin saw them, there's no telling who else did too. "Don't remind me. I hate when she does that shit. It's childish, man. But anyway, how's things with you and ya boy. Getting ready to tie the eternal knot?"

"Not eternal, only till death do us part. After that, his ass can go." She looked back at me to see if I was laughing at her joke. I was still focused on the progress of the breakfast and doing a bad job of pretending to be interested in what she had just said. Selfish, I know.

"Honestly, I don' even know, Shawn. Some days we straight. Other days we're back at each other's throats. Lewis starts actin' stupid when he drinks. Like he gets all controllin'. I been tryna give him a' bit mo' space lately, hoping he could just get his mind right. Maybe miss me a lil' bit. That'd be nice."

I nodded my head with a ninja-like focus on the stove top.

"Oh okay, well that's good then. I hope it works out for yal. So, how much longer till the food's ready?"

"Did you even hear what I said?"

"Sure I did."

"Then what did I say?"

"You said Lewis can drink if it's controlling his throat. Look, it's hard to listen on an empty stomach. Can we eat first, then catch up?"

She turned around giggling to herself. "Boy you so crazy."

After dining and dashing, I went back to my apartment to salvage what was left to reorganize. Even though the place was still empty, I wanted to create a system built for a single man in his own castle without anyone there to dictate where to put things.

It was a lot different setting up the bathroom without the *his* and *her* sides of the sink. There wasn't much in the closet either except the old wire hangers they sneak in your bag when you go shopping for clothes.

In fact, there wasn't much in the house, period. It didn't have a personality to it, or a family feel, just an open space with pictures of Danielle and I that were about to come down. But a sense of pride swept over me. A lot like getting your first car; even though it may be a junk yard special, it's all yours.

The fridge was all mine too, and that's where my independence stopped being fun. I was already thinking about what I was going to eat, and seriously considering cooking for myself wasn't even an option. Jazmin must've read my mind because a few hours later, I got a dinner invite I simply could not refuse. After vacuuming the spaces now left empty and neatly putting my things away, I didn't waste any time at all.

I went back over to Jazmin's apartment. She had a different t-shirt and panties combination this time with light make up and her hair down. Maybe she wanted to make up for the unpreparedness of my previous visit, but I didn't care. I could always appreciate a little effort from a woman to look presentable.

Regardless of how fine Jazmin was, there was none sexier than the meal she had laid before me. Grilled curry shrimp, coconut rice, macaroni and cheese, biscuits, and steamed vegetables. If God was a chef, his food would smell the same way hers did.

We ate, drank Kool-Aid, and laughed over immature topics we should've known better than to all night. It felt just like old times.

"No, Jazmin, no! You're not getting off that easy, answer the question. Would you, or would you not cheat in a race against a physically handicapped person if it was for a million dollars and you were losing?"

"Ha-ha NO! That's crazy, I don't care how much money was up for grabs, that's foul and you know it."

"Oh, so you get a few years of college education and you too good to cut corners. Me? I would trip the hell out of Tink-Tink. I'd never be allowed to another Special Olympics as long as I lived. But I'd be rich."

"Oh whatever, okay this conversation is over. Do you want another plate before I put this up or not?"

"No, I'm good now, thanks. I enjoyed that. I almost forgot how good your feet taste in this food, girl. You gotta keep 'em out the pots or start charging for em."

"Thank you, actually it's my mom's foot you tastin'. I used her recipe and slow-cooked it a little longer than usual. Was you going home tonight or did you want me to bring you out some covers to crash on the couch?"

I didn't expect her to give me the option to stay. I wasn't in any hurry to leave with the 'itis' from my full stomach setting in, and I didn't have much at the house to run back to anyway.

"Well, I don't know what's better, the couch or the bed I got at home that's missing sheets and a comforter. She took those with everything else."

"Okay, so I'll bring you some covers and Lewis got some shorts and a shirt you can sleep in too. Just put your things in the hamper AFTER your shower. I know damn well you ain't thinkin' you bout to be on my couch in all that filth?"

"No, no, of course not," I said, pretending I had thought about it. I was all about being clean, but it was a little less of an incentive if I wasn't expecting sex that night. Most men feel the same way. They just won't tell women that.

"Aight then, well go ahead and take yours, and then I'll hop in when you done. Don't stay in all night either. Leave some hot water for me."

"Won't even take me five minutes." If anybody knew something about taking quick wash-ups, it was me.

Her bathroom looked like it was straight from the TLC channel. She didn't miss a single opportunity to let her personality show, from a matching toilet-seat cover and hand towels with her name stitched in both, all the way to the decorated medicine cabinet.

The bath-tub knobs were confusing me at first. You'd think the color-coded stripes above the knob would help, but I would have much rather seen a switch for an on/off function and a dial for temperature. Like a thermostat.

I kept the shower short and sweet so I wouldn't overstay my welcome. I knew there were more meals where that one came from and didn't want to miss any in the future. I put on Lewis' shorts she gave me, but I didn't realize just how small this guy was. It must've been how brothers felt back in the '70's who had to play in the NBA damn near flashing the fans every time they jumped up.

I couldn't fit my arm through a single sleeve of the t-shirt and gave up before I ripped it or came out looking like I went shoplifting in the Baby Gap. When I came out to see she had made the couch up with sheets and a few pillows, it was music to my eyes. I was so tired, a drive home was out the question even if I did want to try and thankfully I didn't have to answer to someone for where I was going to be. While I was getting comfortable, Jazmin was jumping in the shower. I closed my eyes and felt my internal organs going into auto pilot while the couch cushions gave way to my body. As soon as I started dozing off, I heard her calling my name from the bathroom.

"Shaaaaawn,"

"What?!" I yelled, hoping that I'd either get a "nothin'" or silence in reply.

"Can you come here please?!" *Great.* As soon as I warmed up the couch, I had to leave my hard work.

"Yeah, what you need?" I said walking up closer to the bathroom door.

"Can you look on the bed and grab my towel and robe please? I forgot to bring it in here. I'm not used to having guests."

I don't know why, but for some reason it bothered me to actually be referred to as *guests.* Just three years ago I was making her scream my name and now I had been reduced to just "guests". But whatever. I went into the bedroom and grabbed her pink flowery robe and towel.

She heard the door open. "Just set it on the counter. Thanks."

I walked over and set the robe down. Glanced over at the shower curtain. Even though it was foggy, it was still see-through enough to make out Jazmin's silhouette and a few features like soap suds and nipples.

From the looks of things, her body had matured. Her hips were a bit wider, but her waist was just as small. It looked like she had been in the gym lately. Not running and starving, but lifting heavy, mostly squats. She deleted her unwanted curves and put a caps lock on the rest. Out of reflex, I was grabbing myself the longer I analyzed.

Not being able to see through the curtain in high definition mixed with hormones unsatisfied in months sent my body into an all out temper tantrum. I left the bathroom quickly and went back into the living room.

The couch wasn't comfortable anymore and my sexual frustration was all too obvious in the gym shorts a few sizes too small. I pulled the cover over me and lay on my stomach, refusing to be obvious or even hint at being sexually aroused. It'd make everything awkward and with me being fresh out of my own relationship, she'd be nothing more than a rebound. Had too much respect for her to go that route.

Our friendship was the last thing I had going steady and I wasn't about to ruin it. If I could just sleep it off, I'd live to fight another day.

My alarm was being rude and disrespectful, waking me out of what had potential to be a great dream. I tapped around the floor until I felt my phone. I had the mutant ability to unlock my screen and turn off the alarm without opening my eyes. After a few minutes of being in denial, I accepted the fact that my day was going to have to start eventually, so I got up and scanned the living room for my clothes to see Jazmin walking out of her room, fully dressed with her keys on her way out.

"I put your clothes at the foot of the chair and food is on the stove. Make sure you lock the bottom lock on your way out," She said, closing the door.

I looked over and reached for my clothes from the day before, now neatly folded to perfection and smelling like fresh-scented dryer cloths. Peeked over to the stove and saw a full breakfast spread laid out alongside two ham sandwiches in Gladware bowls. She had washed, dried, and folded my clothes, cooked breakfast, packed me a lunch, and got ready for her own classes. Without waking me up.

I could see why Lewis was in a hurry to put a ring on it. But the hospitality still didn't outweigh the feeling of waking up next to Danielle. As much as I hated to admit it, I was missing her.

She was wrong, dead wrong. But I knew I could've handled the situation better. I had never cursed at her before. I wasn't thinking about how stressed she could've been from work and school. People say things they don't mean all the time, but a part of me couldn't buy into her not meaning what she said.

Maybe she didn't mean to say it how she said it, but her words came from somewhere, and if that place was her heart, then we had a problem.

I refused to be the one taking the first steps to reconcile; it was either she make a move or our separation was permanent.

Seeing her on campus was like a poker match; both of us looking into the eyes of the other to see who was going to fold. I wasn't working with a full house, but I wasn't going to let her know that. I was pretty sure she felt the same. We were two people who wanted the same thing, but both of us were too afraid of coming out and saying it.

My days got longer and I couldn't focus on anything for two seconds without replaying the fight. Every now and then, someone would ask how I was feeling, and I had perfected the "I'm fine and you?" lie. Sometimes it's easier to just fake a smile instead of telling people you're torn up. But I got tired of pouting, and reality set in that I was financially on my own again. I had to figure out what to do about the bills because they never took a day off.

Student loans were foreign to me since I went to school on a full athletic scholarship, but from my understanding, I could still get them if I wanted. Most of my peers used them to ball out at the mall, or pretend to be a rapper for a week, or fold it all up for a little Facebook photo shoot. My needs and common sense weren't going to afford me those luxuries.

I had maybe a week's worth of clothes in my entire wardrobe, no dishes, no food, and no bedding. Sallie Mae was notorious for preying on people in these types of situations, but I had no choice.

I filled out the paperwork for a couple thousand dollars, enough to get back on my feet, and began plotting on more ways to bring in more income. There was no way it was going to last me the rest of the semester, so it was time to go job hunting.

That turned out to be as much of an occupation as the actual job I was trying to get. I went to every fast food joint, grocery store, clothing department. Hell, I was even about to go donate sperm. Luckily I came to a breakfast diner full of women that was short of a man to sexually harass, and I fit the bill.

"Hello, may I please speak to a manager?"

"I am the manager," said the lady at the front register in her bedroom voice. She had this creepy ass twinkle in her eye and scanned every stitch in my zipper as I walked in. I guessed her to be in her early to mid 40s, short, and heavy-set with curves in all the wrong places.

"Oh great. Well, I'm Shawn Fletcher and I was wondering if you were hiring for part-time?"

"It depends. What are your skills?" she said as she faintly stressed the 's' at the end for an uncomfortable two seconds.

"Um, well, I've never really been a cook or anything but I work very hard. I'm always on time, and I'm a quick learner."

"A quick learner, huh?" She looked back at the other waitresses who started snickering. All of them were rough on the eyes, and that much was clear from a distance. I was scared of what I'd discover up close. "Well, we could definitely use a quick learner with your, um, *qualifications*. As long as you're not too quick that is." She snickered to see if I caught the joke. I kept a straight face to pretend I didn't. "When can you start?"

"I guess I can start this week. But don't you want an application first?"

"Right. Come a little closer." I wasn't sure where this was going and I don't remember it being a part of the hiring process. "I'm not going to hurt you, come here."

I got closer to the register just within arm's reach, and she put her hand on my chest, felt around some, then poked at my arms.

"Your application looks and feels good to me. You hired. Be here tomorrow night at 10. You'll work the overnight third shift. If that's okay witchu?"

I had every right to be offended, but I was more relieved to have finally found a job. The overnight shift sounded tiring, but I'd rather be tired than broke.

"Yeah, sure, I can do that. Is there a uniform or something?"

She licked her lips and moaned under her breath. "Well, you don't have to wear anything.....in particular. I'll have your uniform here and you can change in my office or wherever you feel most comfortable."

"Right. Well, okay then. I'll see you tomorrow. Thank you so much. I won't let you down."

She mumbled something I did my best to not hear as I felt her eyes go straight to my ass on the way out. But, I was hired. That's what mattered.

Lean On Me

If I knew how much money waiters made, I would've started a long time ago. I left work with at least $100 every day, mostly in ones which earned some judgmental looks when I went to the bank to make deposits. I'm pretty sure they assumed my income had something to do with a stripper pole and neon orange thongs, and I can't say it was much of a difference between the work environments. I was still objectified like a piece of meat every day, but so long as my faithful female customers were good tippers, it worked for both of us.

The hardest part was working overnight. I was lucky if I got three hours of rest. Sometimes I would go to class still in my work apron, and I began struggling at football practice. My manager was kind enough to give me days off before the games on Saturdays but not before I winked or gave her some other false hope that would suffice as a bribe.

I had never worked so hard in my life, but independence made the exhaustion well worth it. Yet, I could never stop thinking about Danielle.

I wasn't stuck playing love songs on repeat, but in the back of my mind I wondered if she was okay. Financially, I know she wasn't missing me, but who was watching her back on her way from work? Who was helping her relax after a long day? It scared me to consider the real possibilities so I snapped out of it and went on with my day.

Figured I better start investing that energy into reconstructing the relationship with my mother. I had always been a Momma's boy so I wasn't going to stay mad for very long. Besides, she had long since apologized for acting out of panic the day of the fight with Mr. Macklin, and then left him not too long afterwards.

Whether it was for her own good or not, I knew it was still bothering her. I could hear it in her voice how sad she had become when I called her before class every day. That in addition to my own broken love story was all the more reason to refocus on my first priority, family.

"Good morning Momma. You woke?"

"Yeah, I been up. Gettin' ready to head out to the office and make some phone calls. Hopefully I can get a closing on this property."

"Ah, don't worry about it. I'm sure you'll get it. Guess what. I got an email from an agent after the game Saturday. I looked him up and he's legit. He signs players to NFL teams every year for huge contracts, and while he didn't say it directly, he seems really interested in me."

"Oh really? That's nice. Did you email him back?"

"Nah"

"Why not?'

"I can't. Not yet anyway. It's against the rules. He was probably just tryna get first dibs, in case other agents had their sights set on me. I heard they're like sharks out there. What else you doin' today besides work?"

"Well, I gotta go by the leasing office and try to get an extension."

"Extension?"

"Yeah. These folks harassing me about this rent money I don't got. That's why I need this closing."

"Hold on. So you late on the rent? How much you owe?"

"Don't worry about it. Once I get this closing I won't owe anything. Times is tough for everybody and they charging for gas like it's pumping from the fountain of youth. Can't nobody catch a break, especially me. Hell, I'm tryna sell a house and I can't even buy one my damn self."

"Momma, tell me. I got a few dollars you can have if you need it to hold you over till you get the closing."

"No, you keep your money and keep doing what you're doing. I don't need you worrying about me. I can handle myself."

"I know you can, but I'm asking you to let me help you. You would help me if I needed it, right? You can't be an example of something you don't want me to follow. Now how much you need?"

"400 dollars."

"Wait, is that the full amount? You don't have even a part of the rent?"

"That's including the late fees. I was late last month too. It's just a rough time for me and I'd be damned if I ask Greg for a dime."

"Oh you and Mr. Macklin not even talking anymore? Well, all right. I got you. I can send it today so tell the landlord you got it."

"You don't have to do this, Bud. I'll get an extension on it and pay it later. I want you to focus on that schoolwork and your football." She was the only one I let call me Bud. It was a childhood nickname I had from resembling Kenny, a.k.a. Bud, from *The Cosby Show* as a child. I worked hard to live it down after puberty but I couldn't stop her from saying it.

"Look, I'm sending you the money. I gotta go now. I'm about to be late for class. I love you and drive safe."

"All right then, baby, I love you too and thank you. I'll pay you back as soon as I get it I promise."

"I don't need you to pay anything back. You're my mother. Now I'll talk to you later. Bye."

Her financial situation had slipped my mind until then. Coincidentally, we were in the exact same boat, newly on our own, and I wasn't going to let either of ours sink. Vicariously, it was my responsibility to assume the role of the man in her life now. A part of that was to see to it that she had what she needed. I've never felt the pain of having a baby but if it's anything how it sounds then she more than warranted a little help in hard times.

I didn't realize how competitive I was until I caught myself getting passionately involved in cooking competitions on the food channel. You never can really tell how good the food tastes; you just have to trust the ability of the TV hosts to look convincing enough that the food in their mouths was really good.

I still accepted leftovers if Jazmin had them and made more time to hang out with her in between time. I could be my own cook, but I couldn't be my own friend. I mean I guess I could, but not without a padded room.

My point is, it was nice having someone to talk to regularly now that mine and Danielle's social interaction had been starved by our pride. I wasn't interested in trying to find another relationship to get into, but I was all for having someone to vent with so that my thoughts had an outlet. We both needed someone to listen to our problems since her and Lewis were on the rocks too.

"I don't know what it is about y'all. One second you're the sweetest people ever and the next thing you know, y'all tryna tell us what we can and cannot do while doing less than you did to get us in the first place. Why is it that? Why do you change once you have what you say you've always wanted?"

"Well, first off, Jaz, complacency is natural for those who've only been taught how to get as opposed to how to get and then keep. In life we've become pursuit-oriented, so once the pursuit's over, we either stop or find something else to pursue. Every how-to in the media is about how to get what you want. When's the last time you heard a rapper talk about how well he's able to keep his girl?"

"Well, if rap music is Lewis' relationship guide then I should've reconsidered a long time ago."

"No, that was an example. I'm just saying, maybe he's not that bad of a guy. He probably just needs a little lesson about keeping his woman. It's not too late to learn that and I think you can be the one to teach him."

"But how? I'm no expert."

"You don't have to be an expert. You're his woman, and if you two are really in this thing together then you have to help each other grow. Sit him down. Let him know how you feel and explain how you want it to work for the long term. Be clear about what you will and won't tolerate. You deserve that much."

"Shawn, you don't know Lewis like I do. He gets defensive when I try to talk to him about stuff like this."

"Then soften him up first. Don't do it in the heat of an argument. Do it during a really nice dinner. Your food can make anybody pay attention. So, make sure his guard is down and also that you're respectful about it. Hey, if he's smart, he'll listen. You're a good girl. Anyone with sense would want to hold on to you."

"You know what? You right. I do a lot for him and I know deep down he loves me. He just has one hell of a way of showing it. But I'll try it. So anyway, how's the single life treating you? You back on the prowl yet?"

"Prowl? I ain't no thirsty ass prowler. If I want it, I'll get it. There's no prowling necessary," I said, pretending I had it all under control. She saw right through it.

"Okay, I can't even front. This single shit is overrated. I'd like to be over Danielle, but I'm not. I'm trying to let logic take the lead on this one because I know better, but my heart. My heart ain't tryna hear that shit. But if I'm the one who tries to work things out, then what? She knows she can do whatever she wants and I'll just come running back."

"Shawn, what she said was way out of line. While she might deserve a second chance, you do deserve for her to be the one to ask for it. So yeah, if you go back, it'll send the wrong message. You gotta wait, and see how things play out."

"Yeah, I know, that's why I'm holding out. Besides, I got other things on my mind. Momma's up to her neck in bills and it ain't gettin' no better. 50 years old, still working three jobs tryna make ends meet. That shit aches me just thinking about it. I know if I can impress the scouts at the combine this year, I'll have a real shot at getting into the league, but I can barely focus long enough to train with everything that's on my mind. I just...I don't know what I'mma do."

"Well, you know if you need anything, I got you Shawn."

I needed to hear that. Everyone needs to hear that at some point, but more importantly I needed for it to be meant and I know she did. I couldn't believe I found myself defending her man which was the reason for us becoming strictly friends in the first place. I guess this was me growing up.

Jazmin solidified her position as a real friend, and you don't get too many of those. Even though she still had a bombshell figure, I wouldn't do anything to jeopardize her happiness nor her respect for me. I thought it was impossible to turn an intimate relationship into one that was completely platonic, but I did. We did.

Just Being Friendly

It wasn't long before I got a peace offering from Danielle. She sent it in the form of all the things she had repossessed before she left, neatly placed in bags outside my door with a note attached that read:

Dear Superman,

I hope it's still okay that I call you that. I just want you to know that I'm sorry for being childish. I should have never taken back the things I gave you, and if you don't want them then that's fine, but they're your things to do with as you wish. I don't care about any of it. I care about you. I care about us. If there's even an ounce of you that still loves me, please, let's give it another shot. I made a huge mistake and I'll prove to you that I learned my lesson if you can find it in your heart to forgive me. I miss you so much. Either way you're a great guy and I couldn't have asked for a better boyfriend. Whoever it is you decide to be with will be one very lucky woman.

Sincerely,

Danielle.

I wasn't thrilled about getting my apology as a note, but I was more relieved that one of us took the first step. I was tired of pretending I didn't care and more so wondering if she did.

I wasn't concerned about getting the belongings back, but it was nice to know she wasn't planning on making some kind of "Waiting to Exhale" scene by burning them on top of my car. I took them in the house and put them in the back of the closet in case I decided to donate them later. Using any of those things she took from me and gave back again was out of the question.

After a few moments to figure out what I should say, I called her.

"Hello?"

"Hey....what's up?"

"Umm...hi. I didn't think you were gonna call," she said, her voice soft and surrendering.

An awkward silence found its way home in an already awkward situation. Both of us trying to let it set in that we were communicating and this time it wasn't at each other's throats.

"Yeah...well, I saw the note that you wrote. And as for the things, you didn't have to give them back. You know that was never the issue."

"I know it wasn't."

"They're just things. The issue was having to do without you. Emotionally. Mentally. When I lost that, I lost the best part of you, and that's what I want back. All of you. But not if you're gonna be on the same shit. I can't do that again."

"Superman, I'm so sorry. I always wondered if you were too good to be true, but I knew that trusting you was the only way to even give us a chance. I got to talking to them because I felt like they were my friends, and I was proud to have a guy that wasn't like the ones they dated, but instead they just made me feel stupid and naive. That's my fault. I shouldn't have listened to them. I promise, I won't let that happen again."

"They didn't make you. You let them."

"Okay, you're right, I let them make me feel that way."

"I'm not tryna fuss at you, Danielle, but I want you to understand the control you have to own over your own feelings in order for us to move forward. Nobody can make you do anything."

"Okay. I understand. I'm not going to fight you on this. You're right, and like I said, I promise I won't let it happen again. I'm so sorry and I love you."

"I love you too."

Once we exhausted all of our pride, communication was easier than ever. No more trying to read each other's mind and body language while our mouths worked just fine to say how we felt. No cussing spree as both of us stood our ground. Just two people, tired of being tired, and ready to get things back to how they used to be.

Apology accepted.

After we cleared the air and got everything out, things quickly got back to normal, maybe even better than normal. Both of us realized that we had been taking each other for granted. Every hug, every kiss, and every time we made love was more intense, literally as if it could've been the last chance we had to do so.

We agreed to schedule quality time every week that didn't conflict with our work schedule so that we could put our relationship at the top of our priority list where it belonged.

There was still one issue; Jazmin and I had revived our friendship those past few weeks, and I was going to have to spend less time with her to make sure I didn't neglect Danielle.

At least, that's how it was supposed to go. You get in a relationship, you're supposed to cut off all ties with other females or at minimum put them on a back burner that never lights up. But her and Lewis' problems had gotten serious, and we both had been leaning on each other to make it through the rough patches. I couldn't bring myself to leave her hanging just because I had gotten my shit together, and at this point, I was valuing the few friendships I had in my life, including hers. In the interest of loyalty, I decided to try and make it work. For everyone.

Telling Danielle the situation would've been the right thing to do for sure, but there's no way she'd understand that I was trying to be there for another girl in her time of need, especially since she knew about mine and Jazmin's history together. I don't know of many females who would. Even though we were working on our trust, that was too much to ask of anyone. If things worked out the way I hoped, Jazmin and Lewis would be back on track soon, and we could all go back to our separate lives to live happily ever after.

Yeah. Right.

I was leaving football practice the next day, and as I was getting in my car, I received a text message from Jazmin.

Shawn, you got a minute? I really need to talk to you.

I didn't want to reply yet since I was supposed to be seeing Danielle in about 10 minutes. I figured I could text her later on in the evening once I went to work, but sure enough, she was calling. It had to be important.

"Hello."

"Hello, Shawn? I'm sorry for calling. I know I just texted you, but I really need to talk. Are you busy?"

"Nah, I'm not, but I'm about to be in a little. You all right? You sound like something's wrong."

"No. I'm not all right. Lewis threatened me."

"He did what?! Threatened you how?"

"He threatened to beat my ass if I ever raised my voice at him again. I had the talk with him like you said and it worked. I told him I didn't like the way he got defensive and that I needed more attention and he agreed. Then today we got into it. I'm not even sure what it was about. But he called me a bitch and I told him not to call me a bitch, and that's when he said he'd beat my ass if I ever raised my voice at him again. He even pinned me to the wall when he said it."

"Jazmin, that's not cool. Is he still over there? You need to leave him alone. You don't deserve this."

"No, he left, but I don't know if he's coming back or not. He usually just comes randomly when he feel like it, but now I'm scared. I think he really might hurt me. Can you just come over here?"

"I can't do that. I had made plans tonight and promised I wouldn't break them."

"Shawn, just this once. I'll even cook for you."

"I'm not hungry, Jaz. I'm sorry, I can't come. Not this time."

"I never ask you for a damn thing and just this once, I need your help."

"Jazmin. I-"

"Shawn. Please. I won't ask you for anything else. I promise."

It really sickened me to keep telling her no. It was my fault in the first place for telling her to try and work things out with him. I couldn't leave her hanging.

"Okay. All right, I'll be there in a few."

"Thank you. Really, I appreciate it."

"Don't mention it," I said, pressing the *END* button.

I'm not sure what was worse; her being in trouble or the fact that I was really about to let Danielle down by breaking our plans. Conveniently, she was working on being more understanding, and if I ever needed it before, I needed it then.

I opened up the contacts and saw Danielle's name. Closed my eyes and pressed the call button.

"Hey, baby," she said in a *I just got paid* kind of happy tone.

"Hey, um whasup?"

"Nothing, waiting on you to get here. The food's just about done now, only a few more minutes. How far away are you?"

I gritted my teeth and inhaled. "Well, here's the thing. I may be a little late if I get there at all before I go to work."

"Oh no, how come? You said this was our time and that nothing would interrupt it."

"I know, and I'm so sorry. Something came up and I gotta go see about it real quick. One of my friends is in trouble and I gotta make sure they're okay."

"What friend?"

"Oh, you don't know him. He's on the football team." There went my lying ass reflexes again.

"Oh, well all right. I understand. I'll just make you a plate to take with you. Just let me know if there's anything I can do and be careful."

"All right then sweetheart, thank you and I will. Talk to you later."

"Okay bye. I love you."

"I love you too."

I could hear the disappointment in her voice, but it was too late. I'd have some serious making up to do, but I couldn't let Jazmin down. She really didn't ask me for anything, so for this one time, I had to come through. I pulled up to her house, still with two hours left before I had to go to work.

Knock knock "Who is it?"

"It's me."

I could see her looking through the peep hole first so I put my nostrils up to it.

"Ha ha, only you would do something so nasty. Get your damn nose off my door, boy," she said, opening the door.

"Well, I'm glad to see you're smiling. You had me worried for a minute." I sat down on the couch expecting to see more signs of a domestic dispute. But her apartment looked as neat as always. A touch of Febreze was even in the air.

"Well, yeah, I'm smiling now that you're here. I really do apologize for making you stop whatever it is that you were doing. I wouldn't have called you if it wasn't an emergency though."

"I know, it's all good. We all need people to have our backs sometime, and I know you'd do the same for me. Not sure how much safer I'd feel, but I bet you could pinch somebody or at least yell for help."

"If your big ass needs help, there ain't nothing I can do."

"Yeah whatever, I guess you got a point. But listen, Jazmin, there's something I wanted to tell you."

It was time to set the record straight. I didn't think Danielle would understand, but Jazmin would have to even if she didn't want to. My main obligation was to my woman.

"Okay but before you start, are you sure you not hungry? I already cooked and since Lewis ain't here I can't eat all this by myself." No sooner had she said that before I felt my stomach growling. "I made my secret recipe fried chicken and homemade waffles. I even cut up a fruit salad to go along with it," she said licking her fingers and looking over at the stove top with pride.

My soul said yes. But my mouth said, "Um, I'll pass, I was about to go home and eat in a little." I was already crossing the line by lying to Danielle. I'd be flying over it by coming home with no appetite for dinner. "Back to what I was saying. I'm going to be here for you, you know that. You were there for me when no one else was and I can't thank you enough. But me and Danielle are back together and we're working things out. So, I gotta do what I gotta do to make this work. I ain't leaving you out to dry, but I'mma be spending more time at home now and I just wanna let you know."

"What are you trying to say exactly?"

"I'm *saying* this can't be a regular thing Jaz. I can't do this and keep her happy too. At some point she's gonna get suspicious and I know for a fact she wouldn't like me coming over here. Don't matter what it's for, the reason won't be good enough. Not in her eyes anyway."

"Oh. I guess I ain't think about it like that. Yeah, if I was ya girl I wouldn't be too happy about it either. I respect where you're coming from though. Well, just chill for a little while longer while I get in the shower, then you can go back home to your wifey. Can you do that?"

"Yeah sure, that's not a problem."

She went back to the room and I heard her turning on the shower. I noticed myself getting a little paranoid as the cars that pulled up outside in the parking lot could possibly be Lewis coming back. I pondered what'd happen if he actually came back to see me there.

In a fist fight, I'd have the advantage. He was a little shorter and a lot slimmer. But surely it'd be even worse for her especially if he was planning on making good on his threat. I couldn't be there for her all the time, and 911 calls automatically got directed to the campus police station which, more times than not, would be ignored by the lazy ass security guards who were sleeping on the job.

She needed a way to protect herself, some kind of weapon. The pawn shop in Auburn was about 15 minutes away and had a huge selection. I could probably stop by and get her one for cheap. I'd feel a lot better knowing she had some line of defense even without me.

A few minutes later she came out of the bathroom with her head wrapped in a turban-like towel style. Her bathrobe was thin, probably made of silk, and it was obvious she had on absolutely no clothes underneath by the detail of her nipples through the front.

"Okay, I'm done now, and sorry for taking so long. I haven't shaved my legs in forever, and I couldn't wait another day without shredding my bed sheets at night when I tried to go to sleep."

"It's cool, I didn't even notice. But okay then, I'll hit you up tomorrow to check on you," I said, getting up and heading to the door.

"Thank you. Shawn you don't know how much it means that you did this for me. Danielle is really one lucky girl."

She reached up around my neck and hugged me, making her body rub against mine. The robe she had on did nothing to put any material between us. It was time for me to get the hell out.

I got home about 15 minutes before I had to be at work to see Danielle in the bed sleep and a plate on the stove. Her food wasn't the best since she never had to cook growing up. We usually had chicken tender sandwiches for dinner, or spaghetti which was her specialty.

I appreciated the effort and dared not to complain because I knew she was trying. I was the lucky one. I grabbed my work apron and the plate and headed out the door. Another night, another dollar. The grave shift was waiting for me.

The next day, I hit Jazmin up to see how things were. She assured me she was fine and thanked me again for being there the night before, but I still felt uneasy about her being alone. I had always tried wiping my hands of problems that weren't mine, and I always failed miserably. Some would commend that, but compassion causes stress. Stress I could do without. I needed to get her something to protect herself to alleviate me of that burden.

I headed out to the pawn shop to see what they had in stock. I never had been a fan of weapons but I'm even less a fan of a woman living in fear, particularly a woman who was my friend.

On the inside it looked more like a garage sale.

No organization, just an array of random products that were marked down to a good price and gently used. I went up to the front counter, and the guy sitting behind it had to be the sloppiest looking grown man I'd ever seen.

He was in need of a haircut, both on his head and in his nostrils. He saw me walk up out the corner of his lazy eye and stood up, his hairy stomach hanging out the bottom of his shirt and pressing up against the counter.

"How can I help you?" he said in his deep, scratchy voice. His teeth looked like he only brushed them with his finger and the odor from his mouth was so strong, I could almost see it in the air when he talked.

"Well, I need something. A weapon."

"Who wants a weapon? You? What do you need a weapon for? You got muscles everywhere."

"It's not for me. It's for a girl."

"Oh I see. If you say so. You got ID?"

"Yeah here it is." I pulled it out and handed it to him. He looked at it for a while, then pulled out some kind of infrared flashlight.

"You're only 21? Geez, I thought you were at least 30." He handed it back to me. I made a mental note to sanitize it later. "Well, you gotta be 25 to buy a gun."

"Who said I wanted a gun?"

"Well ,if this is really for a girl, what else would she need? Anybody could take a knife or a bat from her and we don't carry pepper spray."

"Well, how come I have to be 25?"

"It's the law. I didn't make the rules."

"I don't have to be 25 to get shot. Why do I have to be 25 to shoot? That doesn't make sense."

He looked up as if in deep thought and scratched his cheek stubble.

"You know what? You got a point. Look, I'll let you buy a gun, but you didn't get it from me. Anything happens and I'll swear I've never seen you in my life. How much money you got?"

"I got a $100 dollars. I need something that's not too hard to handle and that's safe. Nothing rusty or real heavy."

"Hmm…..let me see." He walked to the far side of the counter. I could see his ass cleavage out the back of his pants as he bent down to the lower drawers and regretted the split second it took for me to turn my head. "This should do it." He came back over to the counter with something wrapped in a black cloth and set it down.

"What's this?" I asked, unraveling the cloth.

A little wave of glee spread over his face. "Glock 26. It's about as close to handgun perfection as mankind will ever get. It has all the best qualities of the larger Glock models that are brought together to make a concealable 9mm to fit the hand of most shooters well, particularly girls. It can shoot any 9mm ammo you give it with a smooth trigger. Like butter. You're not going to find a much better piece than this."

"Where did you get it?"

"You're asking a lot of questions. You some kind of cop?"

"No, I was just curious."

"Yeah yeah, you want it or not?"

"I need bullets too. Give me some bullets and you got a deal."

"You don't get free bullets and I'm already giving you a huge discount. I'll give you one bullet. Hope your little girlfriend has great aim or more money because that's all I'm giving you for $100 dollars."

"She's not my girlfriend. But aight. Here's your money." He snatched the money and put it in his pocket. I could've sworn transactions were made with a register these days.

"Remember, you never came here, kid."

I'm not a kid, I thought to myself as I walked out. That conversation didn't need to go on any longer, and I wasn't too keen about walking around with a gun on me. I didn't have a license, and I didn't know how to use one which was more than enough reason for me to stay away from them.

I went and put the gun in the trunk of the car. I could drop it off at Jazmin's later since mine and Danielle's next scheduled quality time wasn't until tomorrow. For now I needed to get a quick nap in before I fainted. This whole working-all-night, stressing-all-day routine was getting to me.

Later that evening, I swung over to Jazmin's apartment right after practice. I hadn't told her about the gun yet, because I didn't want to weird her out, but this was for her own safety. I wasn't making myself available to be her personal security guard anymore, but I did care about her well-being.

Knock Knock "Yo, Jaz, it's me. Open up." *Knock knock knock knock knock knock-*

"Boy, what the hell is wrong with you beating on my door like you crazy?" she said as she flung the door open with her neck rolling from side to side.

"You sound startled, which is exactly why I came over here. May I?" I invited myself in past her still holding the door open in anger.

"What you mean? I thought you said you couldn't come over here so often because you wanted to be home for your girl. It's the next day and you back already?"

"But I come bearing gifts and I'll be right out of your way soon. Look, I know you've been really on edge lately with the whole Lewis situation. And since I can't always be there, I got you something to keep you safe in the meantime."

"I don't want a dog and I already have a whistle."

"No, no, no, I have something even better." I pulled the gun out my book bag and set it on the table still in the cloth. It made a soft clunk and I could see her body shift when it did.

She squinted at the gun as if she was trying to see through the cloth and said, "Shawn...what is that?"

"Take it out and see."

She cautiously went over to the table and pulled the cloth back. When there was enough of the gun showing to reveal what it was, she jumped back onto the couch.

"What the hell! Is that a gun?! Whatchu doin' with that thing?!!!" She yelled. For this to be something we could both get in trouble for, she wasn't exactly using her inside voice.

"Okay, I know you're probably not used to one of these, but I think it's best if you have one just for emergencies."

"Shawn, I ain't tryna kill Lewis. I don't know how to use a gun and I don't even want it near me. Take that back wherever you got it."

"Whoa, nobody said nothin' about killin' nobody. You're overreacting. I'm just saying you can have it for protection. You'll probably never have to actually use it anyway. Once you feel threatened, just show it and I'm sure he'll go the other way. It's better safe than sorry."

"Yeah, but nothing is safe about having a gun in my apartment that I don't know how to use or even have the nerve to. Where did you get this and why is there only one bullet beside it?"

"I got it from the pawn shop down the street, but that's between me and you. And I couldn't afford to buy bullets so he threw that one in for free."

"Yo cheap ass. You gon' get me a gun with one damn bullet. I guess if I missed, I'd just have to throw it at him, huh?"

"No, Jaz, and now's not the time to be funny. The point is, you feel threatened every day and that's not fair to you. Everyone has a right to protect themselves and this is giving you your best chance."

"No."

"No what?"

"I can't do it. I know you mean well but you gotta take that back or give it away because ain't no gun about to be up in here. I'm sorry."

"Don't tell *me* you're sorry. This is for you."

"I know, and I appreciate it but I don't believe in guns. I had too many bad experiences with them, and I swore a long time ago I'd never use one."

"What? What you mean, too many bad experiences?"

She looked away and I could see memories that she didn't want to come back inviting themselves into the moment.

"My dad used to be a cop. And he used to beat my momma's ass every day whether it was for an outfit she wore, or just because. Any reason was good enough."

"Jazmin, I'm sorry. I had no idea."

"And when he used to beat her, my brother would try and help and he'd beat him too. He was only 12. I was 10," she said, tears collecting in the ducts of her eyes.

"You really don't have to talk about this if you don't want to. I should've never brought it up."

"He beat him like he was some nigga off the streets. A grown ass man balling his fist up and punching a child in the face. And then one day, I couldn't take it and I screamed for him to stop. He came over to me and asked me what I was going to do if he didn't. Then he handed me his cell phone and told me to call somebody and if they came over, he'd kill them."

"Why didn't you just call the police?"

"So what? His cop friends could come over, and turn the other way like nothing happened?"

I just sat and looked at her instead of continuing to drive my foot in my mouth.

"Look. Shawn. I don't need no gun. I just don't believe in em."

"Alright. Say no more. I'll hold on to it."

Say My Name

The bomb she just dropped was leaving debris in my thoughts for the rest of the day. I had no idea it was coming, but it made me want to help her even more. I had never been in a situation like that, but I can only imagine how helpless she was and how it must be making her feel to be in such a similar situation now.

I thought that at first, she would've accepted the gun out of pity alone. Kind of like when you drew your mom that really crude picture in kindergarten but she hung it on the fridge to let you know she appreciated you for trying. But I just felt like a complete ass for not only getting her in this situation but then making it worse. Some knight in shiny armor I was.

The next day was finally my chance to make amends with Danielle for the previous time I bailed out on us hanging out. I had been putting her on the back burner and she didn't deserve it. With all of the speed bumps and curvy roads dealing with my mom's situation, and especially Jazmin's, it was time to get something in my life on cruise control so I could try and remember what it felt like to exhale.

I needed another plan. I didn't give this one a name since the last plan I named failed me miserably. Names were bad luck.

I was still writing in my free time, just like I always had since I was a kid. Poetry was my first love, but short stories were my new passion. I had been working on one about Danielle and I as somewhat of a log in my journal, documenting all of the things we'd overcome; so I split it up into chapters amongst four "just because I love you" cards, one for every chamber of the heart. It was time to step my game up.

I gave her the cards throughout the day, each with a rose and a kiss to make sure I built up her anticipation and curiosity. I could tell she knew I was up to something, but she played along with it. At first.

I limited all casual conversation and small talk, only giving her direct orders via text messages on where to meet me to receive the next chapter of our story. I think that bothered her a bit, but she still cooperated.

By the time I was giving her chapter 3, she completely gave up on trying to hide it.

"You know, Superman, you can just tell me what this is all about," she said, smiling.

I refused to break character. I stared at her blankly.

"So you're really not going to talk to me? All right, fine. I won't try to get you to talk anymore."

Her reverse psychology still wasn't enough. I blinked a few times, expressionless and staring.

"Superman, please just tell me what is going on already. This is not fair." Her face was beaming with hopeful anxiety. Just the way I planned it. I handed her the rose and the third card. I went to kiss her on her cheek but she grabbed my face and tried to put her tongue on my Adam's apple.

This was it, I had her. After the kiss, I walked off without saying goodbye. My thoughtful segue to what was about to be a very hot and steamy night was almost complete.

I got home about an hour before she did so I could clean up and remove any fragile items from the bedroom. The nightstand lamp, all of the pictures hanging up. I even moved the bed off the wall a few feet so the headboard wouldn't put a hole in it. The room was now jungle-sex proofed so all I had to do was leave the final chapter where she could find it, drink my Red Bull, and stretch.

I heard her come up to the front door of the house and pause to read the final chapter from the card. This one concluded:

...And the two were a match made in heaven. But until God had their homes ready,

they made their own paradise on Earth using <u>love</u> as the foundation to help them weather the storms,

<u>trust</u> as the security system to keep the intruders out, and

<u>lust</u> as the home cooking to make their stay a little more worthwhile.

THE END.

P.S. Come into the room and don't..... you... say.. a word.

She opened the door, and before she could turn the lights on, I grabbed her hand gently to lead her in.

"It's okay, I got you," I whispered. We walked into the bedroom, already set up. "Almost there. Now, lie down and just relax. I'll take it from here."

The fact that she wasn't resisting any let me know that she was down for whatever I had planned. That got my adrenaline flowing. I went over to the stereo and pressed play on the slow jams' playlist. *There's A Meeting In My Bedroom* by Silk dropped that classic baseline at the beginning of the song and their voices filled the room. It was the perfect soundtrack for what was about to take place that night. I came back and undressed her, starting from her feet and working my way up from there.

As I was taking off her socks, I could see the screen on my phone lighting up. It was on silent and her eyes were closed so she didn't see it. Whoever it was could wait. I refused to let this plan be a repeat disaster of the last.

I proceeded, slowly caressing her, monitoring her increasing heart rate as I teased all of her hot spots. I kissed her toes, massaged her calf muscle, and kept working my way up to undo her zipper.

A few seconds later, I saw my phone ring again. *Damn, can I get some privacy* I thought to myself, but I was too curious to keep ignoring.

I moved on to the other side of the bed to get a better look, now removing her shirt, and I could see the calls were coming from Jazmin.

Figured. I knew she'd think twice about having the gun around so she could feel safe, especially since it was night time. But I tried to help her and she didn't want it. I could still give her the gun, but it was going to wait till the next day. My time wasn't hers to do with as she pleased. She would just have to get a night light this time.

I put the phone on the floor and slid it under the bed with my foot. This was time for Danielle and me, and for once I needed to keep my promise to her.

I kept going, touching, and kissing her frame. I felt the energy from the Red Bull creeping in and I was fully erect to the very tip. It felt like I was reinforced with stainless steel, freshly cooled from the fiery furnace and casted into a slight curve to the left.

She melted in my hands, letting me have my way.

I couldn't take it anymore. I pulled her to the edge of the bed, put her legs over my shoulders, and converged our bodies. My eyes rolled back.

She gasped.

Put her hands on my thigh to keep me from going too deep, too soon.

Her lips were soaking wet, wrapping around me, kissing every vein all the way back to my pelvis and as sure as she opened wide, I was filling her up.

I kept pouring.

Her body shivered when I was in far enough to reach that spot at the very end of a woman's vagina to let you know it was no more left; which was perfect because I had no more left. She fit me like a glove.

In between eyes rolling in the back of our heads, we caught glimpses of eye contact.

There was so much passion in hers, a slight fear, but trust that no matter what, I was going to be taking care of her. Just the way I wanted it.

I pressed her legs toward her ears and leaned all the way over like they did in the *Smooth Criminal* music video. I felt her holding her breath, biting her bottom lip. That let me know that I was hitting her G-spot and every other letter of the alphabet she had in there.

I got cocky.

"You feel that, baby?" I said, daring her to talk. It was something we didn't do a lot of. Our body language alone was like poetry.

She nodded her head and moaned.

I eased out and then dove in deep again, this time swirling my hips, digging around for gold. I did that for another five minutes or so. The playlist was on about the sixth track. I heard Jodeci's *Freek'N You* come on.

That was my shit.

It was time for me to turn up.

I slid out until just the head was in and then pulled her back into me a little faster.

Further.

Reaching for dear life.

Then I did it again.

And again.

She was only breathing in between the strokes. Short, quick, and controlled breaths.

Another 10 minutes went by and I could feel the sweat beading up on the end of my nose, but I had found a steady rhythm. The V cut of my stomach was meeting the V-shaped opening of her legs at a place called Ecstasy downtown.

The headboard was slamming the wall with the weight of my body thrusting into her.

We didn't care.

I gave myself permission to pick her up.

I rarely did this since football practice kicked my ass. Besides, Danielle wasn't exactly skin and bones. A solid 170 pounds curved to perfection under a smooth, mahogany lamina . But I was built to handle every bit of it.

I slowed down to a grind and let her legs fall into my biceps so she could reach my neck. I felt her fingers lock into place like the seatbelt of a roller coaster does before it takes you on a ride.

I stood up again, both of my hands clenching her ass, swinging her into my body like a pendulum.

Her moans turned into screams so loud it drowned out the music. I could tell I was going deeper. That stop sign at the end of her vagina was starting to hurt, but dammit I was late for work. There was no stopping me.

I kept going, faster, deeper. No signs of fatigue. The sweat between our bodies made the smacking noises louder.

About five minutes in, she sang, "I'm 'bout to come, Superman." It sent my adrenaline through the roof and I grabbed her ass tighter, speeding up, maneuvering with more aggression.

I felt her legs locking up around me and she screamed like I was giving her the winning lottery ticket. Her orgasm was consuming her, and exciting me.

Her screams gradually went back to moans and then subsided to her trying to catch her breath again. I laid her down on the edge of the bed and pulled out. I felt her trying to roll over like we always did when we were done.

I said, "Where are you going? No. Where do you *think* you are going?" still standing over her, as profoundly erect as when I started.

"I'm...but...wait...what's going on? We just did all that, and you want even *more* pussy?"

"Little boys get pussy. I get stomach. And yeah, I want more."

By the time she tried to open her mouth to form a word, it was too late. I was already on one knee, tongue deep between her thighs.

What was supposed to be her sentence turned into a mumble. A pleasant one.

Her back arched and I felt her hands on the top of my head.

Kelly Rowland's *Motivation* was playing now. I even bobbed my head and flicked my tongue inside her to the rhythm of the beat. Kelly Rowland had a beautiful voice, but it was nothing compared to the notes my baby was hitting for me.

I felt myself getting my second wind. I still had yet to come, but that wasn't my priority. She was.

I kept licking in and around her vagina, down to her ass, and back up again.

I saw her hands clench the sheets and her toes popped from curling so hard.

"*Shit,*" she groaned, as her body jerked.

I growled on her clit, reaching down with one hand to make sure I was still at attention.

I stood up again, my face glossy.

"Turn over,"

She obeyed. Eyes closed, she rolled over and asked, "What you tryna do to me..."

"And stop talking." I said.

"Mmhmm," she moaned, smiling with her eyes closed.

I got on the bed and closed her legs so I could straddle her. One hand reaching to grab the headboard and the other guiding myself into her.

Home training went clean out the door and locked it behind itself.

My alter ego was making an appearance. He was fresh out of prison and a menace to society.

Once I had my balance, I took my hand off the headboard and put it on her neck and put my other hand on her lower back.

The length of me reintroduced us, and the slapping of her ass against my waist was applauding our return.

"*Shit..... Shit... Shit.. Shit,*" she yelled getting louder every time. "I'm about to come again."

I went harder and faster and faster. Driving reckless. No license.

No time to waste.

Damn near airborne.

I felt my body tensing up.

Caught a glimpse of us in the mirror that was on the dresser. I could see the streetlights peeking through the blinds, hitting the highlights of my back muscles and the curve of her ass. It turned me on even more.

I was getting ready to come, and I tried to hold it in. She screamed.

I went harder. She lost all regard for our neighbors and screamed some more.

My abs tightened and I couldn't hold it.

I took the lead, she sang along, and there we were. Harmonizing and enjoying the pinnacle of physical chemistry we'd only heard legends about.

I pulled out. I said something, not sure if it was actual words, but it was vulgar. And honest.

A few moments later, I relaxed back onto my knees, panting.

I stepped back onto the floor, knees damn near buckling, and went and grabbed us a few towels. She still hadn't moved from the position I left her in.

That night was a soliloquy. I knew I had put it down by the first two words she said when we were done.

"You okay?"

"Yeah, are you okay?"

"I can't feel my legs. But fuck ém. I'm better than okay. I'm magnificent. You was in me like you had something on your chest though. Damn boy."

"I mean, I did. I needed you to know that you still turn me on. And that one time of me bailing out wasn't a reflection of whether or not you have my attention. Baby, you have my full attention. Besides, I had to make it mine if it didn't already have my name on it."

"Well, your name is all over it. Cursive writing. Size 14 font. Double spaced and everything, your name is on this. Felt like you was tryna put your name on my stomach too. Did you grow?"

I couldn't keep back the grin. "Pretty sure I have."

"Is that right?" She said laughing. "Well, don't grow no more or I'm cutting you off. You're not about to tilt my uterus."

I didn't even know you could do that. Instead of trying to figure it out, I just left the compliment be and pulled her closer.

I didn't have enough energy to finish the conversation anyway. I was spent. My sex game was usually pretty exceptional. I was young, healthy, athletic, not overly endowed but enough so that I wasn't ashamed to go free-balling in some sweat pants on occasion. But this time, I outdid myself. It felt like I had a crowd cheering and Rocky Balboa himself in my corner, telling me I could do it.

It was electric yet exhausting. People who claimed to do that day in and day out were either liars or didn't have a day job.

I woke up the next morning. My phone's alarm was unwelcomingly reliable once again, but I couldn't stop it because I couldn't find it. I forgot I had kicked my phone under the bed the night before and was still half sleep, not to mention pissed that I had to get out the bed without a few minutes to adjust.

Reaching under the bed and feeling around, I finally found my phone. Pressed the dismiss icon to make it shut up. I wasn't prepared for what I saw next.

87 missed calls. All of them from Jazmin.

But there was only one voicemail. I knew something had to be wrong. I called my voicemail to listen to the message.

I could hear her crying uncontrollably with words in between the sobbing. "Shawn.....oh my God, please just pick up.... I don't know what I'm going to do..... I can only see red right now...and I think something's wrong with my shoulder.....Lewis....he came back.....I ran and I fought, but he was just too strong...Shawn....please.....please Shawn pick up....Oh my God...What am I doing...I'm so sorry....I shouldn't be doing this....." *End of message.*

My heart sank and what felt like the Georgia peach formed a lump in my throat.

I started panicking. Jazmin was in trouble.

I had no idea that's what she was calling for the night before. I needed to go over there and check on her.

It was still early and Danielle was sleeping. I didn't want her to wake up just so she could start asking me questions I'd have to try and dodge. But I had to move quickly because she'd be waking up for class any minute so I grabbed my shoes and tip toed out the front door.

Hopping down the steps one leg at a time, trying to get my shoes on, I tried to call her. No ring, just voicemail.

Not a good sign.

I got in the car and sped out onto the highway. That was the longest drive to her house I'd ever taken. I did my best to block out my imagination, but it got the best of me. I was scared for her.

I pulled in and ran up to the door. Knocked a few times. No answer. I walked back outside and looked in the parking lot and didn't see her car.

The voicemail she left was apparently after Lewis had gone, but I was wondering, did he come back?

I went and got back into my car and turned my phone on loud in case she called. Turned the music up full blast, and still it wasn't enough to distract me from her cries for my help in my voicemail inbox. Cries that I had kicked under the bed. Damn.

I felt like a complete jerk and my timing couldn't have been worse.

I got home and opened the door to the smell of breakfast cooking. I walked in the kitchen and saw Danielle still in her underwear but with heels on and her hair slightly teased.

She turned around when she heard me come, then walked up to me; teeth showing, spatula still in hand.

"Hey, baby. A little early for you to be checking the mail, isn't it? You expecting something?" she said as she reached up and kissed me.

"Uh, what do you mean mail?"

"Well, didn't you just go check the mail? I assumed you went down to the mailbox because you left your wallet." She looked on the table where my wallet sat.

"Oh, right. The mail. Yeah I checked it. Nothing important though," I said, lying through my teeth. This was becoming more and more of a habit.

"Yeah, I figured. Anyway, I'm making your favorite; waffles, eggs, and sausage with some orange juice. Just how you like."

"Thanks, babe, you're the best. But, ain't it 'bout time you get to class? You gon' be late."

"Oh no, I'm not gonna make it to class today. Not after what you did to me last night." She closed her eyes for a second in reflection. "I don't know what got into you. It's like you were an animal. I like it. I say the animal stays."

She looked at me again with a little less glow. "Superman, what's wrong? You're acting strange."

"Wrong? Nothing's wrong, I'm just a little sleepy, that's all. You're right, last night was pretty wild. I guess it just took a lot out of me." I couldn't fake very well, but I think she bought it.

"Okay, well, breakfast is just about done so you can go get back in the bed and I'll bring it to you. Tiger. Rawwr," she said, making tiger claws.

I was glad one of us was in a good mood. I expected to be right in the clouds with her but just my luck, life had different plans.

It always seemed to happen that way. You plan a pretty picnic, fresh fruit, sandwich essentials, wine, a nice freshly cut lawn in the middle of a huge park that not many people know about, then sure enough, you realize the weather man didn't deserve his job and the rain clouds come running in despite all your preparation.

Life had handed me lemon after lemon, and the best lemonade I could make was spilling down my shirt.

I was getting stressed again.

I checked my phone. Still no call from Jazmin. Whether I checked my phone or didn't, it seemed like everything just made me more curious as to what was going on with her.

I could hardly enjoy the moment I was supposed to be having with Danielle. She was showing her appreciation for my hard work the night before and doing a damn good job. Breakfast, in what would have been the bed, all while wearing heels and sexy underwear.

I couldn't catch a break, but I didn't need this to trickle over into my relationship any more than it already had. I sucked it up, found a smile to wear, and continued on with my morning-after treat. But my mind was everywhere except the same room I was sitting in.

I came out of practice later that day to see a missed call from Jazmin. I had been wondering all day when or if she would finally get back in touch with me. Surely she saw my missed calls and unless she was pissed off about me not answering, I at minimum expected an update on her condition.

I was about to leave my locker, and then I caught the tail end of a conversation going on beside me from some of my teammates.

"Man, that boy Lewis done messed around and caught a charge," one of them said.

"Shit, how that happen?" the other replied.

"You know that crazy ass braud he be with? Jazmin?"

"Jazmin with the fat ass?"

"Hell, yeah, her. They got into it. She tryna say he put hands on her. Had the police out there 'n' shit late as hell."

"That's why you can't fuck with these females out here bruh. They gon' stay gettin' ya caught up."

"Shit, yeen gotta tell me. If anything we doing, it's smashin'. That's it. Niggas be tryna wife ém up and shit like this happen. Won't get me."

They split ways and headed to the showers.

I didn't want to return the call in the locker room with everyone around. Clearly she was the front page news on campus, so I hopped in the shower and came back to grab my things. With my scalp still soaked, I made it outside and called her back.

"Hello," she said calmly. That put my mind at ease.

"Hey, Jaz, I'm sorry I couldn't get to my phone last night. I didn't hear it ringing...are you all right? What happened?"

"Yeah, I'm better now anyway. I apologize for that message, I shouldn't have left it. And...honestly I don't even want to talk about it. I just need to take a break to think things through for a while. Everything's happening a little too fast."

"Jaz, it's me. You can talk to me about anything. Look, I'm on my way, just let me in when I get there, okay?"

"Okay cool."

I usually had a grace period of about 15 or so minutes before Danielle's mind would start inquiring on my whereabouts after practice. She knew my work schedule like clockwork, even helped me remember when I needed to be at work sometimes, so I knew I had to be sharp.

The sex we just had gave me a bit of a leg to stand on but even that wouldn't be enough if I got another strike. I pulled into Jazmin's complex and saw her car parked and the lights on through her window.

I knocked a few times.

"Hey, it's me."

She opened the door, and it took every bit of self-control to keep my cool. Her eye was swollen shut on the left and bloodshot red on the right side. Her face was discolored from the bruises, and her lip had a gash on it.

I lit up with anger for the bastard who was responsible and filled with sympathy for her at the same time. Despite all of that, I calmly walked in and took a seat.

"So...you're not going to say anything?"

"What you mean?" I said. I wasn't sure exactly how to lead with the conversation. Everything was moving so fast in my mind and there was no particular place I could start that would make any sense.

"About me being all beat up. I know you see it."

"I mean, yeah, I see it. It looks like it hurts. Does it?" I had a knack for asking dumb questions.

"Yeah, but it's not that bad. The doctor said they'll all heal up in a month or so. Gave me some meds to take in the meantime. I should be fine."

"When did you go to the doctor? You drove?"

"Yeah, I drove. Who else was going to drive?" As soon as she said that, there was this awkward silence that pointed at me.

"Jazmin, I'm sorry. I didn't know what was going on last night or I swear to you I would've picked up. I put that on everything. I had no idea."

"It's okay Shawn, it's not your fault. I had it coming anyway. I should've known better than to pick a fight with him. He's fucking crazy and I knew it."

"No. That's not your fault. It doesn't matter what you did, he should've never put his hands near you. He's a coward. Man, I wish I coulda been here. These dudes stay tryna put their hands on females, but when another guy the same size approaches them, they won't even speak out of turn."

"Calm down. Really, it's fine. I survived and I reported it to the police. There's a restraining order and a warrant out for his arrest. He'll get his eventually."

"So what exactly happened? Did he randomly come and bust down the door or what?"

"No, he didn't. He asked could he come over, so I said sure. We started talking and it started out as an apology on his part. But it was half-hearted, like he wanted me to apologize too. But come on, that ain't no real apology if you're only doing it to get one out of the other person. So I told him that, and I guess it offended him. He got in my face about it, and this time I didn't back down. I always back down, but not this time. I stood up to him. Finally."

"So then what?"

"What do you mean, *so then what*? What do you think? He beat my ass."

"No, I mean like what happened afterwards? Did the neighbors call the police or something?"

"Actually, no they didn't. I guess they were all sleeping or maybe doing what you were doing."

"Look, Jaz, I said I was sorry. You know I would've been here had I known."

"Calm down, I'm just messin' with you. But he missed on one of his punches so I slipped out and ran into the bathroom and locked it. Eventually he gave up on yelling and waiting on me to come out. So he left."

"Well, you wouldn't have had to run had you had the gun."

"I would have to run...from the law. My ass would be on First 48 right now asking for a bottled water and my lawyer."

"Your ass would also be seeing out of both eyes without the red tint too. Jaz, just take the damn gun. If not for you, then for me."

"I told you before, I'm no killer, and that's exactly what I'll be if I had a gun. It's some bitches I already can't stand, I wouldn't even make it to Lewis before I used up that one bullet you gave me. And God forbid I really need it and drop it. I'd be out of luck for real then."

I couldn't believe that she was still refusing to have protection on her as she talked through a sore jaw and blinked through bloodshot red eyes.

"All right, Jaz, you got it. I'm out. I gotta get back home. I know Danielle's about to start getting curious."

"Yeah, wouldn't wanna be tardy now would you?"

"What's that supposed to mean?"

"Nothing, Mr. Defensive, take a joke."

I walked out feeling some type of way about her comment. It's kind of like the same thing your homeboys do when they're trying to make you feel stupid for staying out of trouble. But I should've expected that.

Jazmin was never a huge fan of rules or following protocol anyway. That was the biggest difference between her and Danielle. That 'friends with benefits' shit would never fly with Danielle, whether she was looking to be in a relationship or not.

She wasn't into any lingering friendships after intimacy. I admired that about her; the way she was always so emotionally responsible. When I was a teenager, I followed my heart blindly into a lot of pain, but Danielle paid attention to the road signs her mind gave to keep her heart out of danger. Even though Jazmin and I were more alike, Danielle was the perfect balance for me, and that's why she was the one holding my heart.

I got home to see her curled up on the couch in a scarf, wearing one of my t-shirts, eating homemade cookies and watching some drink-throwing reality TV show. She was picking up a habit of snacking more often lately, but the last thing I needed was to initiate a "you have to love me for me" argument so I let her do her thing.

"Hey, Superman. How was practice?" she said as I walked in.

"Long. Coach's wife must be holding out on him because he drilled the shit out of us today."

"Well, maybe if he stops spending so much time with y'all, and more with her, she wouldn't be so stingy with it."

"Hold on, where'd that come from?"

"Nowhere, I'm just saying." She kept a straight face and continued chewing the cookies. "You hungry? I made one of your favorites tonight. There should be enough spaghetti to last us a week this time.

I made a huge pot."

"Oh, you shouldn't have. Thanks. I was starving." I don't think she realized just how often she cooked spaghetti and just how fast I had gotten tired of it. It used to be once every few months, but now it was damn near bi-weekly. "So what's that you're watching?"

"Real House Side Chicks of Atlanta. I missed the last episode, so I'm finally catching up tonight. I can't believe that Jacky had the nerve to pop up on her best friend's man at work. I swear, these side chicks be having main chick emotions then wonder why no man will take them serious. They just have no respect for themselves. It's fun to watch though, so I'mma keep on doing it."

"I'm surprised you even get entertained by that stuff, Danielle. I thought you had too much substance to even tolerate it. Ain't you supposed to be somewhere sitting Indian-style, listening to audio books, and eating leaves?"

"Ugh, eating leaves for what?"

"I don't know, I figured that's what people who listen to audio books do. Seems peaceful."

"Now *you're* the one that needs to stop watching so much TV. I feel like you just subliminally called me a goat."

"Oh, come on now, of course I didn't. But if you were a goat I'm sure you'd be the most beautiful goat in the whole flock, baby." I reached down and kissed her forehead.

"Superman...sweetie.....goats don't travel in flocks. Those are birds."

"Look, you know what I mean. I think that reality TV is making me dumber by the second. Turn to some ESPN. I'm tryna see Lebron and the Heat play tonight."

I went in the kitchen and fixed a plate of ol' faithful, a.k.a. spaghetti. As she promised, there was more than enough spaghetti to fill a kitchen-sized trash can which is exactly what I had in mind, but I knew better.

I couldn't expect her to be outstanding in every category, but I was in lust with the thought as I watched the re-heating plate rotate monotonously in the microwave.

I looked back at the couch and noticed she was completely ignoring my request to change the channel. It was like the reality TV show had hypnotized her into a trance, lowering her IQ with every martini that flew across the table. But I let her have it. With the way I had been coming in late, I didn't have a lot of room to talk so a few sacrifices on my part wouldn't hurt.

I Got You

"Jazmin, I can't. No, as matter fact I won't. I simply refuse."

"Stop being a bitch. You're a big boy, you can handle it. Or can't you?"

"If I eat another piece of that cheesecake, I'm not going to have an appetite for dinner and Danielle's going to kick my ass."

"She won't mind, that just means more leftovers and less cooking for her. Now come on, eat up."

"Okay, if you insist." Gladly, I succumbed to the peer pressure and dug my fork into another chunk of her strawberry cheesecake. The more regular the spaghetti dishes at home became, the tougher it got to witness the greatness that was happening in Jazmin's kitchen without being a part of it.

"Good, I knew you wouldn't resist. I made this one a little different from the last one. I found another spice, normally used for apple pies, and put that into the crust. That and a few other secrets I won't share just in case you feel the need to go back and tell everyone. I might open up my own restaurant one day."

"Yeah? What would you name it?"

"*Jazmin's.*" she said, as if a vision of the actual restaurant just flashed before her.

"Oh, how creative of you. Did you come up with that all by yourself?"

She rolled her eyes and sucked her teeth. "See you always gotta be a hater."

"You know I'm just kidding, Jaz. You got talent. On top of that, you actually enjoy doing it. Most people cook because they have to. Either they got a family, or they're trying to diet or something. But you do it just for the love of it."

"Well, my momma always told me that the way to a man's heart is through his stomach. I don't know how true that is, but I know whoever my man is will be well-fed."

"Yeah, I'm sure. I hope you like 'em chunky 'cause he gon' be fat as hell once he tastes this cheesecake. Your restaurant gon' stay packed."

She looked at me, scanning my face for sarcasm. "You really think that, Shawn?"

"Yeah, man, I know it. Just give me and my family free meals so I can get refuge from Danielle's cooking every now and then." I hadn't fully gotten the words out my mouth before I realized how wrong that was. My heart was the worst when it came to filters, and it was speaking under the influence of the deliciousness that was on my fork.

"Well, maybe you could take some of the pressure off her and do a little more in the kitchen yourself. Why do men think it's the women's job to do all the cooking? I love to cook and I still get tired of it every now and then."

"I mean you're right, but to be honest I'm no Rachel Ray on the stove either."

"Well, I can teach you to cook. That way you won't be over there starving."

"For real?"

"Yeah, I'm surprised you haven't already asked me to actually. While you over here struggling to resist my food, you can just make the same thing at your house."

She had a point. While I was busy being Jazmin's taste tester, I should've been doing more to help Danielle out. It had been a few months since we had gotten back together and now the daily routine of living together was getting tough. Being *the man of the house* was still about teamwork and I wasn't being the best teammate.

"Okay, cool. I'm down. Well write up your recipes for me and I'll try-"

"Oh, no, no, no. You will not be writing down any of my nothin'. That's how stuff gets stolen. Real recipes are memorized anyway. My momma never used a written recipe and neither will I."

"But Jazmin, I can't always be here for you to teach me."

"Don't you want better food at home?"

"Yeah I do, but still I-"

"But nothing. That's probably why she keeps making the same thing over and over again. She wants you to step up and help her out. I swear you guys just have no clue about us."

"Okay, but I don't need a full menu for her to see my effort, do I? A few dishes and we should be good."

"Look, cooking is just like sex. Once you get the basics down, the rest is pretty much up to you and your creativity. And you never were too creative."

I snapped, "The hell that's supposed to mean?"

"Oh nothing. Isn't it about your bedtime? I got a test I need to study for and surely Danielle is wondering where you are."

"If you want me to leave, just tell me to leave. I was on my way out of here anyway." I got up and headed toward the front door, the remainder of my cheesecake in hand. "Tomorrow, 7 o'clock sharp. Let the cooking lessons begin," I said as I walked out.

I doubt Danielle was curious about my whereabouts. At least that's what her actions were saying. She was acting strange lately, distant almost. She had gotten more and more wrapped up into TV and everything at home just became a mundane routine.

Long, passionate French kisses turned into pecks on the cheek as we parted ways in the morning; lazy ass "it gets the job done" sex every now and then, and that damn spaghetti.

We still talked, but even the conversation had been reduced to the habitual "Hey, babe, how was your day" conversations as I rambled, she nodded, and then vice versa. Then she would run off to her reality TV shows and studying, and I'd either go to work or sleep.

Danielle and I not only lived together, but we also had the same classes, so the few minutes I did spend at Jazmin's house after practice became a breath of fresh air. She was my only friend, outside of Danielle, and ever since the incident that led to our "break", Danielle made me her only friend.

Naturally, things got a bit stuffy, but I supported her efforts to rectify our trust by avoiding miserable females who wanted company. So I kept my mouth shut and hugged her through it as usual.

One night, I came home and I noticed something was different. Danielle was really starting to pack it on. Her stomach, her thighs, and everything else had noticeably gotten bigger.

In my eyes, she would always be beautiful no matter how big she got, but what worried me was where this pattern of behavior was coming from, or better yet where it was leading to.

I saw her in the living room on the couch. This time the TV was off, but she was still watching it. "Babe...what's up. You all right?"

"Yeah, I'm all right, why?" she mumbled.

"You don't sound all right. Baby, you do know the TV is off?" She looked away as if I touched a nerve.

"Yeah, I know."

"What's wrong? Talk to me, sweetheart." Even though we were within arm's reach, she continued to avoid eye contact.

"I just don't feel...happy. Not like with you, I just mean in general. I have a weird feeling and I don't know what it means to be honest."

"Okay, so you sure it's not me? Is there something I can do to fix it or make it better or-"

"No, Superman, it's something I gotta figure out." I saw her eyes water before she dropped her head again. "I think I'm just overwhelmed by life right now. Everything is too much. Sometimes I feel like I need a pause button so I can catch my breath. I get sick and tired of waking up every day trying to dodge judgments, discern amongst the fake smiles and greetings, sifting through people's bullshit just to get to the little piece of truth if there's any to be had. Most of all, I'm sick and tired of being sick and tired. I'd love to give all my burdens to God, but I feel like He's the one giving them to me and I don't know why or how much longer I can carry them."

We both paused a moment to let everything she said sink in. It was clear this was something she had been thinking about for a while by the emotion in her tone.

I cupped one of her hands between both of mine and looked her in her eyes. "Baby, that's what I'm here for. Until you feel like you've given your burdens to God, at least let me help you carry them.

Holding it all in is only going to make it heavier on your conscience, and there's no need when I'm right here. He gave you burdens but He also gave you help. You just have to be willing to accept it."

"If it was that easy, I would've done it by now. You know how much I hate complaining, but not everything is so cut and dry or in black and white."

"I'm not saying it's easy, but we didn't make it this far by giving up. It'll take some time, sure, but the time has to pass either way. We might as well spend it working through this together." She looked back up at me. I must've caught her attention. "Look, we can find some hobbies together, maybe start taking morning jogs or dance lessons. Try to work out some of that negative energy and use it as quality time."

"Are you naming exercises because you think I'm fat?"

"No, of course not, you look fine. If you have gained weight, I sure can't tell." I looked at her, trying my best to keep a straight face. I could tell she bought it by the half grin she gave me.

"Well, I think I might have put on a few pounds so working out doesn't sound like a bad idea. Not right now though, let's start next week."

"Why next week?"

"I don't know. It just seems like a good time to start. You can't just start things in the middle of the week. It's bad luck...or something."

"Okay then, babe, next week it is. Can I have a kiss?" She smiled and reached over for another peck, but I turned my head to steal one on her lips. I locked in and grabbed her love handles to pull her closer. I could sense an uneasiness when I touched them, as if she was more conscious of their existence, so I held on.

I wanted her to know that it didn't bother me. That no matter what,

I was going to embrace her. I think we all go through our emotional ups and downs, and it's hard to tell what someone's battling internally by looking at them. But a lot of times, smiles are just knots at the end of the rope we use to hold on a little longer. For whatever reason, things were getting to her, so I needed to make myself more emotionally available for times like these. My love meant that she'd never have a problem again that had her name on it without mine beside it.

But Baby...We Can Still Do This

The next day I called off the cooking lessons with Jaz. While it seemed like a good idea at first, I'd probably have more fun cooking with Danielle and messing it up with her than spending more time away from home to perfect the craft.

Jaz was upset, only because she went out and bought ingredients to do the teaching, but after my promise to pay her back and let her keep the food, she let it go. No sooner had I gotten off the phone with Jaz before I got a call from work. It was the middle of the day, so I assumed it was a mistake.

"Hello?"

"Hey, Shawn, are you on your way?" It was one of my coworkers, not sure which one. I purposely never paid enough attention to any of them to be able to distinguish between their voices.

"What do you mean, 'Am I on my way'? I don't work again until tomorrow."

"Well, according to the schedule, you're supposed to be at work right now, as in one hour ago. She just told me to call you before she wrote you up as a no-call-no-show." A no-call-no-show was grounds for automatic termination. I had military-like discipline when it came to showing up to work on time, but when it comes to cheap labor, that still doesn't get you very far.

"No, there's some kind of mistake. I only work third shift. She knows I have class in the daytime."

"Well, she's the one who told me to call you so it must not be a mistake."

"Put her on the phone."

"She's busy right now. Because you ain't here. So you coming or what?"

"No, I'm not coming. I'm walking into class right now. I can come right after to try and figure out what the problem is. Hello...hello?"

She had already hung up by the time I finished my sentence. Manners weren't too high on the priority list amongst my coworkers and neither was class so I wasn't surprised.

There was no way I could be on the schedule for day shift. I went into class long enough to be counted presented and pretended to excuse myself to the bathroom so I could leave. I wasn't able to concentrate anyway so it was doing me no good to just exist in class.

Having a job seemed like more of a burden than a blessing. It was stressful, and it did a number on your self-esteem when you see people who have everything just handed to them while you're scraping for every dime you get.

Bills will make you do some crazy things.

I pulled up at my job and saw three charter buses in the parking lot. Some soccer teams were on a road trip and just so happened to stop by apparently for a quick mid-day breakfast. I walked in and saw my manager at the front register glaring at me.

"Hey, what's going on? I got a call saying I was on the schedule for today."

"Oh, don't worry about it. I fixed it."

"Thank God, you had me worried for a second. I knew it was a mistake because I-"

"Oh, I didn't say it was a mistake. I said I fixed it." She continued to glare at me with a 'what you gon' do about it' smirk on her face.

"What do you mean? Like you took me off the schedule this week?"

"I mean the schedule is no longer any of your concern because you're fired. If I can't depend on you to come to work then I need to find someone else."

"But wait, how was I supposed to know you changed the schedule? I've had the same work hours for months now and they've always been at night. You never said you were doing anything different with the hours. C'mon you know if I had known to be here I would've come or at least have let you know something."

"It's your responsibility to check that schedule every day to see if anything's changed. You can't go on thinking that everybody's going to baby you and hold ya hand. I swear y'all college kids so spoiled." She curled her lips as if she wanted a reaction. I was still in too much shock to give her one. "I'll need your apron by 3 p.m. tomorrow or it's coming out of your last check."

"What check? We only get paid in tips."

She folded her arms. Clearly she didn't care about the apron. She just wanted to rub it in that she was firing me.

I had never gotten fired before and it was just as fun as I thought it wouldn't be. I looked over and saw everyone lined up in the back snickering and watching us. A part of me wanted to go off on them, but a better part of me knew that one wrong move, and I was going to be in the system dealing with that kind of shit for the rest of my life.

I had something to look forward to in life, they didn't. They needed to get whatever laughs they could get because this was where the buck stopped for them. That reminder brought me back to earth and dealt me a smile.

So, I channeled my inner Chuck Norris as I turned and walked out the door, mentally dedicating my first million dollars to opening up another restaurant across the street to put them all out of work. Bastards.

--

Later that evening, I came home to an empty house. Danielle was working. Normally, I'd be trying to catch a nap so I could make it through my work shift.

I didn't know if I should start rehearsing my lines I'd give Danielle as to why I lost my job or pick up the remote and turn on the TV. I chose the latter.

I flipped through a few shows I'm never interested in: *Home Improvement, 90's high school re-runs*, game shows, etc. After a futile effort to entertain my mind off things, I got up looking for something to eat, and not to my surprise, found spaghetti in the fridge with my name on it. That was my green light to go ahead and whip out the apron and get to work.

I went to pre-heat the oven and looked at the different temperatures. They all looked hot to me so I picked one, then proceeded to picking out what seasonings I'd use.

I was familiar with the basics, salt and pepper, but outside of that was foreign territory. I had cooked before but only for myself in which my only standard of excellence was for it to be edible.

I saw a few seasoning salts, lemon pepper, and other colorful containers I never noticed in the cabinet before. Once I had them all out, I looked to the freezer for the meat and saw some nice, thick-cut pork chops towards the back.

Perfect.

There was no point in waiting for it to thaw, and besides, it could thaw out while it was cooking, so I thought. I tore the plastic off and began seasoning them right away. No need to make things complicated.

I had a pretty good lather of flavor going within the outer coating of ice so I went ahead and stuck the chops in the oven. Not sure if I needed a pan to set them on, but with the way the oven racks looked, I assumed they were designed to be something like an indoor grill, perfect for direct application of my chops.

I set them neatly about an inch apart in the oven. No need for a timer. I pretty much could use the eye test to see if they were done. Everybody knows what cooked food should look like.

I was starting to see why Danielle had made spaghetti instead of the home cooking I longed for; this stuff was not easy.

Since I had done such a good job on the main course, I rewarded myself by being lazy with the vegetables and opted out of a homemade salad for a few sliced pickles. They were just as healthy as any piece of lettuce and prevented cramps too.

I didn't care for rice very much and bread was a lot easier to handle, so it was a no brainer on what we'd do for the grains portion of the dinner.

Pork chops, pickles, and sliced bread; full course bon appetite. All I had to do now was wait. Waiting sounded like a great idea and sitting on the couch and resting my eyes seemed like an even better one.

"Superman, what's that smell?"

"Hey, baby, when'd you get in?" I looked up and saw Danielle standing over me.

"I just got here. Didn't you hear me open the door? Were you asleep or something?"

"Sleep? Nah, ain't nobody sleep." I looked at the clock and saw two hours had gone by. I jumped up and ran to the oven. I had forgotten all about my pork chops. "No, no, noooo!" I opened up the oven and the smoke rushed out, filling up the kitchen

"Superman, please tell me you did not go to sleep with food in the oven. Now you're going to have the whole house smelling like smoke and you better hope that smoke alarm doesn't go off because if it does, then-" Like clockwork the smoke detectors sounded off.

Even when you're fully aware of what's going on, they have a way of making you panic. She started yelling. "Oh my gosh, please, shut that thing up! I told you not to let the smoke alarm go off."

"You act like I asked it to or something. Help me find a towel." We both scrambled around the laundry room for a towel since there wasn't any hanging up in the kitchen. I saw one in the dryer, and frantically started beating the smoke detector with it to stop it from screaming.

I managed to get the one I was working on to stop but the smoke detector closest to Danielle was still going. Quicker than I could say "You might wanna move," I turned around to see the fire sprinklers emerging from the roof in uniform fashion.

It was already too late; Danielle stood helplessly as she was drenched from the top down, all the while looking at me without so much as a blink. I had really outdone myself this time.

So after the fire trucks and policemen stopped laughing at the reason for their false alarm, I mopped up the floor and apologized repetitively until mine and Danielle's empty stomachs started calling for attention again.

"Danielle, I was just tryna-"

"Why was you tryna do anything when I made spaghetti? There's plenty of it left. I know you saw it. You know what, let's just go out and get something to eat. I don't even feel like warming up any food now, much less cooking something else. " She folded her arms and looked the other way in disappointment.

I got up and started towards the door. I wasn't going to argue with anything that meant having a free pass to avoid the spaghetti, even in the wake of me screwing up. She threw on a hat to cover up her freshly blow-dried hair and headed out after me.

We were silent the entire walk to the car so I assumed that meant the decision of where to eat was on the driver, me. So I played it cool and went to this wing spot downtown.

It had a diner atmosphere but fast food prices, which was perfect for living within my means now that I had my new job of being unemployed.

We remained silent during the drive as Danielle's head was buried in her phone the entire way. She had been getting more wrapped up into social media and reality shows, so it wasn't long before the social apps would stake their claim on her attention as well.

We pulled up to an empty parking lot, both of us looking like 'who shot Jon and forgot to kill 'em, so I wasn't complaining.

Empty restaurants are better anyway; first dibs on seats, quick service, and if there are TV's, you can pretend you're trying to listen to them in awkward moments like the ones I was sure to have.

A teenage, brace-faced blonde-headed girl met us at the front. She looked us up and down as if she expected us to ask her for a quarter then remembered to lead us to a table just in case we were customers.

"Hello, my name is Amanda and I'll be taking care of you two tonight. Would you care to start off with a beverage; maybe coffee, tea, or orange juice?" she said. Amanda sounded a lot nicer than the tone of her body language.

"Yeah, I'll take a water please." I used to be embarrassed to get water because I felt like it screamed 'broke'; which a lot times, was the truth.

Fortunately, I had begun looking like I might be in some kind of shape so getting water for health reasons was my cover in case anyone asked.

I looked over at Danielle who wasn't even paying attention. "Babe...your drink?" I said, staring at her along with the waitress.

"Oh, sorry. I'll take a water too please," she murmured.

Amanda's demeanor turned back into 'aggravated' as she went to the kitchen to fetch our drinks.

"So what's up, Danielle? Tell me how your day was."

"I mean it was okay, Same ole' same. How was yours?" she said, not even breaking concentration from her phone.

"It was cool. I mean other than the cooking part. I didn't go to sleep in any of my classes today. I know you gotta be proud of that. And today was a pretty easy practice. Ready for the season to finally be over though, I can't lie." I looked over and saw her still focusing on the phone.

I went a few seconds of not saying anything, and then she gave an "mmhmm" in agreement to what I said seconds ago. She was listening like a man.

"What's in that damn phone that's so important?"

"Excuse me, who are you talking to?"

"I'm trying to talk to you. I mean, can't you put the phone down for just a few minutes for us to have a decent convo? You can update your status and tweets later."

"For your information, I'm trying to study my notes for a test I have tomorrow, something I would be doing at home if you hadn't tried to burn the house down. Secondly, I was listening to you. I can multi-task."

"Look, I wasn't trying to burn anything. I was trying to cook for us. Don't you get tired of cooking spaghetti? I know I get tired of eating it."

She put the phone down in her lap."If you didn't like my spaghetti, all you had to do was say so." I could tell her feelings were hurt, but the truth was out. No going back now.

"I just wanted to help, Danielle, that's all."

"Well, you've done quite a fine job tonight. As a matter of fact, you can eat by yourself. I'll be waiting in the car. I just lost my appetite." She snatched my keys off the table and started walking out.

"Danielle, wait. I'm sorry, come on now, you know I was just playing wit' you."

She kept walking. The waitress came back out with two cups of water. I grabbed one of the cups and took a sip so her hard work wasn't in vain, then followed Danielle outside.

I got in the car, and put the music on blast to make it clear that I wasn't expecting her to talk. Keyshia Cole was on the radio singing one of her "Niggas ain't shit" anthems so I turned stations to hear more of the same from scorned female R&B singers doing their part to keep women miserably single.

Finally, I turned to some country music where I knew I could at least free myself from lyrical cosigns to Danielle's disappointment in me. We drove for a couple of minutes and then she reached over and cut the radio off. Always a pet peeve of mine.

"I was listening to that."

"Well, I wasn't."

"Look, Danielle, you can be mad all you want. It's your pity party. But this is my car and I said I was listening to it." I reached over and turned it back on.

She turned it back off. "Well you're not the only one in this car and since when have you ever listened to country anyway?"

"I listen to anything I damn well please." I turned it back on again. She looked out the window the rest of the ride and it was clear both of us couldn't get home soon enough.

We got back to the apartment and wasted no time going our separate ways. She changed into her pajamas, something she normally only wore to bed when she was on her period or to signify I could expect no nightcap, and I went and took a shower.

I still had yet to let her know that I was out of work, and at this point, I wasn't sure if I even wanted to let her know. I stayed in the shower long after the last soap suds were gone, just letting the water flow down the back of my neck. It felt like it was rinsing the tension from my body so I could clear my mind; a much-needed stress reliever.

I came out of the shower to see Danielle still glued to her phone.

I looked over at her pile of books in the corner of the room and realized her laptop was sitting on top of them and wondered why she still needed the phone to study.

I wasn't about to ask though. That meant breaking the silence that wasn't completely my fault in the first place.

I mean after all, while I didn't have much tact, what I said about the spaghetti was the truth. I was sick and tired of it. And it wasn't like all I did was sit and complain; I actually tried to help the situation by cooking.

It's not my fault I'm not a chef. She had yet to thank me for any of my efforts so I had just as much a right to feel unappreciated as she did.

I got in the bed, put the covers over me, and turned away from her toward the wall. Usually, I would cozy up behind her and she'd fit her body up against mine; and I would hold her till we either fell asleep or got too horny to go to sleep and had sex.

But not this time. I hated nights like this. They were unnecessary and never fixed anything. I relieved myself of the responsibility to figure it all out and closed my eyes.

I said "I love you" under my breath, purposely low enough to where she couldn't hear it.

No matter how angry we were at each other, I never wanted to go to sleep without at least saying the words because I knew there was no promise I'd have another chance to do so later.

Blurred Lines

"So let me get this straight" Jazmin said, pacing in front of her living room TV. She did this a lot when she had to think hard about something.

"You tried to broil frozen pork chops. Except you went to sleep on the frozen pork chops while they were in an oven at a temperature you're not even sure of, possibly 500 degrees or better. And when she comes home, the house is almost on fire, she gets drenched by the smoke detector sprinkler system, and then you take her out to eat only to diss *her* cooking?"

I looked down at my shoes and swallowed. "I mean, come on, when you put it like that, it sounds worse than what it is. But yeah, that's what happened."

"So what part of 'you fucked up big time' don't you understand? I can only imagine how mad she was. If that was me, the police would've had a little more on their to-do list, starting with getting my shoe out your ass. Especially with the money I pay for my hair, I would've slapped you for every strand of 100% Brazilian Virgin Remy you caused to get ruined. You lucky all she caught was an attitude." She started readjusting her hair as if to make sure it was still intact.

She had some nerve. I hated when females did the whole u-n-i-t-y, we-shall-overcome thing. No matter how wrong they may be, the benefit of the doubt goes to the one with the ovaries.

"First off, she doesn't wear weave. Secondly, how many men even attempt to cook for their woman? I mean damn, can I at least get some credit for the effort? I was trying to do the right thing. It just didn't turn out like I planned."

"You mean the same way she was trying to do the right thing by making sure food was cooked when you got home every day?"

I squirmed a bit at the conviction of the statement. A part of me couldn't argue. The other part said, "You're taking her side now. I just lost my job and all I wanted was dinner with my girl."

"Wait, you lost yo job? How'd that happen?"

I slouched back on the sofa and picked an imaginary spot on the ceiling to focus on. "Long story, but my point is, I'm trying my hardest here. I don't know what I'm doing, I just know what I want to do and that's make this work. Sometimes I don't know if I'm cut out for this. But I love her."

She walked over and sat on the cushion beside me. "Have you told her?" This time her tone was much softer.

"Of course, I tell her I love her every day."

"No, I mean that you're thinking about leaving her."

"Whoa, I never said I was leaving her. I just said I didn't know if I was cut out for it. Doesn't mean I'm giving up, I'm just...I don't know, man." I got up, went to her fridge and poured me a glass of vodka. No ice, no chaser. Yeah, that's how I felt.

"Well, maybe you should reconsider being in a relationship if you feel like you're not ready. It's not giving up, it's just seeing if it's what you really want. I mean how will you know if you just continue stressing? Nothing will change unless you change it."

I took a sip and realized I either underestimated the strength of vodka or overestimated my strength to drink it straight. I came back and sat on the couch next to her. "So you're suggesting I break up with her? Even after you just said she deserves to be mad? I'm confused, Jaz."

"Well, I want you to be happy. It's sounding like she's not making that happen and regardless of whether or not you were wrong, that's a problem. You do a lot of dumb shit, but you deserve that much. You're not a complete asshole." She cracked a smile as if she was hoping for me to return one. I wasn't in the mood.

"But I'm part time? Gee thanks, you really got a way with words, ya know?"

"You know what I'm saying. So okay, back to the subject. Do you really wanna make things right or what?"

"You know I do."

"Well, do something about it. You've never had a real relationship outside of high school and this. You don't know whether or not you're settling for less or if you're really messing up a good thing."

"What are you getting at here?"

She focused her eyes slightly away from me. I could tell she was losing confidence in whatever point she was making, but I was still curious to know.

"What I'm getting at is, maybe stepping out of the situation will help you get a broader perspective. In the meantime, you should try at least one more fish in the sea, just to make sure it's not you that's the problem."

"Nah, Jaz, you talking crazy. I'm not with the whole experimenting thing, not when it comes to love. Our relationship is serious, not some case study."

"I get all that, Shawn, but you can't even think straight right now. You said yourself, you don't know if you're ready for this. So what if you're not? You keep trying to force it, it's only gonna be worse for both you and her at the end of the day."

"What happens when she goes and tries another fish in the sea, huh? What happens when that fish is better than me and I lose her because I 'couldn't think straight'?" I felt myself raising my voice a bit. The thought alone was scaring me.

"Well, you know what they say. If you let something go and it doesn't come back, then it was never yours to begin with." Not only do I not know what 'they' say, but I don't know who 'they' are and why 'they' are qualified to give me life lessons.

"I can't risk that. I know I'm not a bad dude, but I also know any guy would love a chance with her. This is one lesson I don't wanna learn the hard way. I wouldn't be able to stand to see her with another man."

Jazmin paused for a second, pursed her lips, then set her eyes directly into mine. "Has she been acting strange lately? Is she a bit moody more than usual?"

"Yeah, sorta."

"Has she been on her phone more often, sometimes at odd hours? Or right after a heated argument?"

"Yeah, she has," I said, wondering where she was going with this questionnaire.

"Then yup."

"Yup what?"

"Another fish is already swimming in her sea," she said.

I stood up. "Jaz, that's not funny and I'm not laughing."

"You need to wake up, Shawn. What, you think you're the only one unhappy wondering if this is for you while she's at home twiddling her thumbs? More than likely she's feeling the same way, and from what you told me, she's already taking action."

"Nah, not Danielle. She wouldn't do that. I know she wouldn't."

"How come? Because she said so? Yeah, that's pretty solid evidence."

I got up and headed to the door. She rushed over and put herself between the door and me.

"Shawn, I know you're frustrated right now. I've known you for years and I can tell when something's bothering you. But you have to do what's best for you and that's find out where you stand with this before it goes on any longer. You could be trying to force this while someone else out there is a better fit for you," she said, looking at me, getting close enough that our noses could almost touch.

It was then that I realized what was going on. She was coming on to me. Her whole demeanor had changed.

I had never known her to be the one to throw hints; actually she had always done the exact opposite; very direct, blunt, and without tact. But there was that undeniable look in her eye she had a few years ago when I first met her.

It was mature now, more womanly, but still the same lustful gaze as before. She put one hand on my chest, gently clenching my shirt and focused on my lips as she cocked her head slightly to the side and came closer.

She got on her tippy toes and closed her eyes as she came all the way in for the kiss, and then my reflexes unfroze me long enough to side-step away.

"Jazmin...what are you doing?!" I said, whispering and yelling at the same time.

She opened her eyes again then looked at me embarrassed. "I...I don't know. Something just came over me."

"No-hell it didn't. Nothing ever just 'comes over you'."

"Okay, so maybe I meant to do it, but it felt natural like you wanted it too."

"Wanted what?"

"To kiss me."

"No, I didn't. I thought we were just friends. What's gotten into you?"

"Nothing's gotten into me. You were sending me vibes like that's what you wanted. Why else would you be over here when you and ya girl beefing?"

I stopped a minute to think. She flipped everything around on me in just that short amount of time. "I'm over here 'cause I needed somebody to talk to. Look, maybe it's best if I just leave," I said, going back to the door again. This time she didn't try to stop me.

I got in my car and started it up. The music was still blasting as loud as I had it before, scaring the hell out of me so I turned it off. I sat there, staring back at the door, trying to figure out if what I thought just happened really just happened. It would've been awkward if for whatever reason, she came back to the window to see that I was still there so I pulled out of the parking lot and started back home.

I wasn't expecting that at all. Over the last few years, I had actually started seeing Jazmin as just a friend, nothing more. I even stopped looking at her ass when she walked by which was a huge achievement for me.

Even though I put on a good face while I was there, something about the whole situation didn't exactly offend me. Actually, it turned me on. I loved being dominant in the bedroom, but confidence is always sexy and you need a lot of it to make as bold a move as she did.

In my mind, I was ashamed I even put myself in that situation, but I felt my hormones wishfully-thinking about what I could've done with her. How I had changed in the bedroom so much since we were just 18-year-olds, and I how I could make her recant that statement about me not being *too creative* with just 15 minutes alone and a flat surface...to stand on.

I shook it off, tried to focus. My penis was rising in my football shorts the longer I replayed those last few minutes so I punched the gas to hurry up and get home. Danielle and I had some work to do.

I finally got home and saw Danielle's car not in the driveway. It was getting pretty close to midnight, and usually she was home by then if she wasn't at work, but with all the studying she had been doing lately, I figured she was at the library.

I couldn't do too much thinking since all of my blood was in the wrong head. By this time, my penis was at full attention, so hard you could use it to chop down lumber.

I went inside and cut on the shower, leaving it ice cold. I stripped down, took off my jewelry and jumped in. I felt the goose bumps emerging and my pores tightening as the water ran down my body.

The shock of the low temperature made me shiver but not enough to deter the ambition of my hormones. After two long weeks of not having sex with Danielle, they were being as resistant to going to sleep as is a five-year-old on Christmas eve.

I waited a couple minutes, trying my best not to think of Jazmin. I sang Barney songs, the alphabet backwards, every trick in the book, and when I looked down, nothing had changed. Defeated, I turned the shower off and grabbed a towel. I heard the keys jingling outside the door. Danielle was home.

I rushed out of the bathroom and met her at the door as she walked in.

"Hey, Superman. How ar-" she tried to finish her sentence, but I had my tongue halfway down her throat as I pulled her inside and kicked the door close behind her.

I could tell she was surprised by the look on her face and the awkwardness in the way she kissed me back, but I kept going, expecting her to eventually get the message and just roll with it.

We kept kissing, me passionately taking the lead. Me, still fully erect, making it difficult to walk, so I scooped one hand behind her knees, picked her up, and carried her into the bedroom. I felt her stop kissing me back so I paused a brief moment to let her speak.

"Superman, what is going on? Why are you doing all this?"

"Baby, don't ask questions. Just kiss me." I locked into her lips again entering the bedroom and she continued to resist, reaching for the light switch and turning it on. I laid her on the bed and she looked down at my erection. The look on her face told me that she finally got the message.

"No...not tonight. I just got back home, I need to take a shower. I've been running around all day."

"I don't care about all that. I want you, and I want you now."

"No, maybe tomorrow night, okay? I just don't feel like it. I gotta be up early anyway. It's best if I just try to hurry up and get some rest."

I ignored her and reached for her pants. She knocked my hand away and got off the bed.

"I said no. Not tonight." She had a frustrated look on her face. Something had to have been bothering her for her to turn me down like this.

She pushed through my shoulder and walked back out of the room and into the bathroom.

"You could have at least wiped the floor up. There's water everywhere." I heard her say down the hallway.

I was livid and my pride was hurt, partly because this always looked really easy in the movies, but it had just backfired on me. I wasn't the smoothest guy on the planet, but me being fresh out of the shower usually did the trick in putting her in the mood.

I heard her cut on the shower and considered joining her to give it another try, but cutting my losses was in the best interest of my bubble which had already been busted enough for one night. My flag was no longer at full staff anyway. I guess it felt my pain.

I normally would just whip out the laptop, some lotion, and relieve whatever stress I had that way, but this time there was too much on my mind. I thought back to my talk with Jazmin again, the part where she implied that Danielle was already testing the waters.

Why else would she be acting this way, and coming home late? No sooner had the thought crossed my mind than I heard her phone ringing. It was now one o'clock in the morning; nobody ever called her this late unless it was an emergency.

My heartbeat sped up and I was overwhelmed with curiosity to at least go over and see who it was. Maybe I could even answer and hear the voice.

I started over to the phone and heard the shower water cutting off. I jumped back into the bed and got under the covers. She came in and checked her phone, then looked over at me.

"Why didn't you tell me somebody was calling me?"

"Oh somebody called? I didn't even hear it ring. It must be on vibrate."

"Yeah, but no biggie."

"Well, who was it? It's pretty late for someone to be calling. I hope everything is okay," I said, holding my breath for her answer.

"Just one of my students I'm tutoring, probably begging for my text book still. Some people just refuse to help themselves ya know?" she said, still drying off. She kept towel blotting her hair as she rummaged around the drawers for clothes to sleep in.

I felt relieved. I really had started letting my insecurities get to me. Even though I was still horny and unsatisfied, I was happy. Jazmin didn't know what she was talking about.

I had enough drama for one night. Sleep was calling my name and I refused to ignore it.

Furthest Thing From Worth It

"Good morning, baby," I said, bending down and kissing Danielle on the forehead.

"Oh my God, what time is it?!" She popped up out of bed. She was always the one to wake us up in the morning unless she was morbidly late for something.

"Relax, relax." I said handing her a cup of orange juice. I was still focused on having some sex pretty soon, and was willing to do any sucking up necessary to get it. "I woke up a little earlier today and decided I'd make you some juice before you headed out."

"Oh...thanks," she said, grabbing the cup from me. "What time is it?"

"It's 5:45. You got plenty of time to get ready, baby. Don't worry. You not late."

"So you mean you woke me up? That's 15 more minutes I could've been asleep, Superman." She set the cup back on the night-stand and threw the covers over her head again.

I could understand. When Momma used to wake me up too early for school, every side of the bed was the wrong side.

I walked back to the dining room. I never woke up this early before and my first class wasn't for another two hours, but I still wasn't sleepy.

I got on Facebook and looked to see if there was any catching up I needed to do. The first thing I saw on my newsfeed was Jazmin going on a rant.

She posted Facebook statuses shortly after I left last night, all of them with just a few minutes in between them that read:

I hate when a friend is so blind to the bullshit, that telling them only makes things worse.

Never put yourself out there with someone who isn't willing to meet you halfway.

The worst thing about making a first move is when that person's next move is in the other direction.

Best friends make the best lovers.

Apparently, she hadn't stopped thinking about the night before either. I heard Danielle bumping around and closed the laptop shut.

She came out of the room scrambling with one shoe on and the other in progress all while she brushed her teeth and carried her books.

"Why are you rushing?"

She kept walking, trying to step into her other shoe. "I got an early meeting with my student this morning to go over some last-minute notes," she said, spitting through the toothpaste still in her mouth.

"Well, let me help you."

She said, "No, thank you, I got it. I'll see you later," and went out the door.

I admired how serious she was about her academics, but I hated when it started infringing on the attention she gave me. Nevertheless, support is all about sacrifice. The least I could do is put my selfishness aside, and allow her room to be great.

Jazmin was still taking her share of mental real estate on me at the moment. I couldn't believe she had the nerve to try and come on to me. Her running in between the door and me. Then telling me I was probably missing out. Then the attempted kiss. It was all too much.

In a way I felt disrespected, but I knew she didn't have ill intentions. Maybe I did send the wrong message by airing out my dirty laundry, but that's what friends do. We take the laundry out, talk about ways to get it clean, and if it works, we fold it and put it away over a few drinks.

It didn't help that she was so damn sexy. Her body was carved from a block of perfection and given just enough flaws to deem it human. My hormones were getting to me again.

I needed some sex, and I needed it fast. Something about testosterone disables men from thinking straight. Either we want to fight when we normally wouldn't, or we want to have sex when we normally shouldn't. I was in that latter category.

I felt my good sense slipping the longer I contemplated the situation; my thoughts went from negative disdain to wishful thinking, more so about the sex than the situation, but nevertheless wishful thinking.

It didn't help that Danielle was going through another one of her sexless spells. Two weeks straight with hardly a peck on the lips. She'd either ignore my erection or dare to break it off if I kept trying to sneak it in while she was asleep. Masturbation had gotten old because once you've had the best, good is no longer good enough.

I went on throughout the day thinking about sex, how I was so close to getting some from a girl I shouldn't have, and then shortly after denied by another girl that I shouldn't have.

Every ass that walked by, every time I could smell the fragrance of a female, even innocent smiles from complete strangers were turning me on. My penis was so sensitive that just sitting in class, feeling it touching my thigh, had me using a book to cover up my stiffness when I got up to walk.

I had it bad. I figured I'd give it another shot with Danielle that night, and if she turned me down, I'd flush my pride and just beg. She was scheduled to be off, and to my knowledge she wasn't preparing for any more big tests.

There wasn't a real reason why she wasn't having sex with me. Maybe I just kept catching her at the wrong time. That gave me some confidence. If I could just hold out a little longer, it'd all be over soon.

Football practice was always a nice window of relief...I could expend plenty of my frustration, but at 22 years old, I always had some to spare.

I was ready to forget about being a gentleman and have one of those "clear the furniture out and stretch" types of nights. One positive thing about being in a drought, is that you learn to appreciate the excitement you get before sex, like you're a teenager all over again.

Danielle still had no idea that I had gotten fired. To keep from telling her, I just kept up my usual schedule of being away from the house, using that time to fill out applications I had picked up earlier in the day when I wasn't at Jazmin's house.

I still hadn't talked to her since the night before and judging by her Facebook posts, that conversation needed to happen. Being that I had been deprived for the previous two weeks, I knew I'd better stay away from her turf. A good man is still a man, and I knew my limits.

So I spent a little extra time going to collect job applications to turn in. I looked at the clock and realized it was almost midnight, a little too early for me to be home, but maybe that was a good thing and I could pleasantly surprise Danielle with some physical attention.

After the sex we were about to have, I knew she'd be glad to have me home anyway.

I started on my way home and saw a missed call from Jazmin. I guess the silence was killing her, but I wasn't expecting her to break so soon.

She'd just have to wait. Instead, I focused on getting back to Danielle so we could clear my mind.

I stopped by a nearby gas station, picked up my Red Bull energy drinks, and was ready to go. Instead of waiting till I got to the apartment, I went ahead and popped one open to go ahead and get the energy flowing before I got there.

I pulled up in the parking lot and saw a familiar car in my parking spot. It looked a lot like the vehicle I saw pulled up by Jazmin's house back when her and Lewis were dating, but I wasn't sure.

There were a million cars like his, and with everything that had taken place, I had gotten paranoid so I dismissed the thought and found another empty spot close by.

I was just about finished with my drink, and turned off my engine to do so in peace, when I looked at the house to see my door opening. What I saw next all but flipped my world upside down. It was Lewis and Danielle standing in the doorway.

I stared, daring not to blink, so I wouldn't miss a thing. They stood there for a few seconds just within reaching distance.

They seemed to be having a few last laughs from a conversation that was coming to a close, as he would mouth a few words and she would laugh hysterically.

She had a look on her face I hadn't seen in quite a while. It was warmer, and with more energy.

Then I saw them hug each other. Not the kind of hug you give your pastor's wife at church, the kind of hug that you expect a woman to fling one foot in the air as the guy spins her around. It lasted approximately 5.5 seconds, four seconds past the maximum for being friendly, and as they came out of the hug, he held on to her hips, looking into her eyes as she smiled back.

I knew what that meant, and without wanting to see what was coming next, I started the car back up, put it in reverse, and sped out of the parking space.

Out of the corner of my eye, I could see that neither of them even noticed my presence or the fact that I was going 40 miles an hour in a parking lot, which made me even more angry.

I couldn't believe it. Well, I could, but I didn't want to. All this time, I couldn't figure out what was going on with Danielle, why she seemed so different. Why she needed her phone so close by her, or why she was always leaving early and coming home late, or why nothing I was doing ever seemed to satisfy her. It all made sense now, painful and brutally harsh sense.

I didn't know how, but I ended up back at Jazmin's parking lot, just staring at the steering wheel. It had become somewhat of a reflex to drive there when anything was on my mind.

I still hadn't talked to her since the day before when everything had gotten out of hand and she tried to kiss me. I wasn't sure if she'd give a shit about my continued relationship troubles, but with it involving her ex-boyfriend, I knew it would catch her attention. So I called her.

She picked up on the first ring. "Okay, so Shawn, I was gon' call and talk to you earlier, I swear I was. I just want to say that I apologize and that I never-"

"Jazmin," I said, cutting her off.

"Uh…..yeah?"

"It's okay. Open the door. I'm outside."

"You're outside?" she asked with her voice rising. Then I saw her come over to the window and peek through the curtain. "Okay here I come," she said, then hung up the phone.

I got out of the car, double checked the locks, then walked up to the already opened door to see her standing in it. She was, again, in the same robe she always wore. The silk, damn-near-see-through one that left little to the imagination and pleasantly so. She was scanning my face to try and read my eyes as I walked past her and into the living room.

"It's past midnight. Why you over here so late? Are you okay?"

"I just...I just needed a place to go. I can't think right now," I said, flopping down on the sofa.

"I mean, but why though? Is it about yesterday because I told you I never-"

"No, it has nothing to do with yesterday. I saw Danielle with another man. She's cheating on me."

She paused for a second then sat down beside me. "Shawn...I'm so...I'm so sorry. I don't know what to say honestly."

"You don't have to say anything. I don't need anybody to say anything. I just don't wanna feel like I'm feelin' right now."

I put the pillow over my face to hide the tears getting ready to form. Hearing myself admit that I was getting cheated on was almost as bad as seeing it happen. I was hurt by Danielle, but my ego was making me more and more angry at the man she was seeing, Lewis.

I'm sure she was only cheating because I had been neglecting her to see Jazmin. I was only seeing Jazmin to keep her safe from his abuse. This was all wrong.

I felt Jazmin's hand gently grab the pillow from my face. I couldn't fight it. The tears had broken free and she was going to see them sooner or later anyway. I sat up and ducked my head so I wouldn't have to make eye contact.

"Shawn, don't cry, it's gon' be okay. You just need to relax for a little, let the dust settle, and you'll be all right. I can't believe this happened. I'm sorry for even jinxing it."

"Nah, don't be sorry. It wasn't you. I just can't believe this shit, man. How the hell I let this happen?"

"You didn't let anything happen. She chose to do it. Her and whoever it was. Did you get to see the guy's face? Did you know him?" she asked, pulling me to lie on her chest, something like a mother does her child.

I thought about telling her who it was, but decided not to. That was only going to switch the subject into something I didn't feel like talking about. "Nah, I don't think I do. It was dark."

"Oh, well, I don't know what I can do, but I'm here for you if you wanna talk about it. But it's cool if you don't. I gotta go finish up some work right now and I'm sure you'd rather be alone so just take whatever time you need and holla if you need me."

She got up and went back into her room. I was trying to take her advice, and just let things soak in, but the more it did, the more angry I got.

I should have never left and just given him the ass whooping he deserved a long time ago. There's no telling how long this had been going on. While I was busy trying to befriend and protect his ex, he was busy fucking my girlfriend.

Beating him up wasn't going to change the truth, but it would have definitely eased the tension. I needed revenge, relief, or whatever was on the menu to fix a bruised ego and a broken heart.

I looked up and saw alcohol on the fridge. I was told that if you drank in times of sadness, you'd turn into an alcoholic. The alcoholics I knew all seemed to be doing better than what I was doing at the moment, so what the hell. I grabbed the closest bottle of vodka and turned it upside down.

It burned a little on the way down, but not so much after a few seconds. I took a breath and repeated two more times then went and sat back on the couch.

I watched the second hand go around on my watch, trying to focus on something other than the memories of the last few hours. After about 15 minutes of being unsuccessful, I was back to looking for something else to hit the spot.

Inebriation wasn't enough for relief and definitely not for revenge.

"Shawn, you all right out there? I don't hear you moving around. You alive?" Jazmin yelled from her room.

It clicked. "Uh…yeah, I'm good," I said, now feeling the buzz of the vodka binge. I wasn't drunk, but it became a little tougher to hit those syllables without running them into one another.

I got up, steadied myself, and made my way to her bedroom door. It was slightly cracked and I could see her lying on her stomach, facing away from me.

She had on another Victoria's Secret laced panty and bra matching set. Her legs were shiny, and the small of her back had those two little dimples that drive men crazy. She looked sexier than ever. I knocked, enough so that the door didn't move too much but that she could still hear it.

"Shawn!" She snapped around, scrambling for her covers. "What you doing? Didn't yo momma teach you to knock?"

"I did knock. Your door was already open. My bad if I startled you, but can I come in?"

She rushed over to the door and pushed it closed in my face. "Wait," she said. I heard her rummaging around in the closet a few seconds then she opened it again. "Yes, you can." She had slipped on her silk robe that she wore when she first opened the door. As she walked back to her bed, I could see the same imprint of her underwear and the curve of her ass through the back that looked even sexier with the adornment of the robe's silk.

"What's up? You still thinking about Danielle?" she said as she sat on the bed with her back against the headboard.

"Actually no, I'm not. I'm tired of thinking about that. I just wanted to come back here and thank you for everything. I've never gotten the chance, or taken the opportunity to just say thank you."

"You ain't gotta do all that. I don't mind being here for you. We all need somebody and I know you'd do the same for me."

"But I want to. I mean, I wanna say thank you. But I also want to do more than just say how I feel and you're right, we all need somebody, but I have a question." I came over to the bed and sat at the edge. I could tell the closer I got, the more uncomfortable she looked. Her guard was still really high.

"Okay...? What's the question?"

"What if I needed you?"

"Shawn, you're just saying that because you're hurting, not because you really mean it."

"But what if? What if I really needed somebody to be there for me, without judging me or asking a lot of questions. Would I be able to count on you?"

"I mean of course, you know you can count on me."

"Okay, so I have another question. Do you trust me?"

"Yeah," she mumbled, still trying to figure out where I was going with this.

"Then trust me. Don't ask questions, and don't judge me."

"Okay," she said.

I reached over and touched her foot for a safe ground to test her nerves. She was still a bit tense, but she was trying to hold back any reaction out of curiosity on just how far I'd go.

I understood the body of a woman. It's a marathon, not a sprint. So I took my time and slowly moved my hand up her leg up to her knee, and back again. I did this a few times until I felt the tenseness gone from her.

"Shawn, what is this? What are you doing?" she said.

"Remember what you told me and remember what I told you. No questions, just trust me."

She curled her lips, slightly annoyed, but she cooperated anyway. I moved my hand up to the lower part of her thigh using it to put a slight pressure on the inside where I knew she'd be a bit more sensitive.

The pressure I put on it reached deeper into more tenseness and I stayed there for a few moments, massaging it out. I looked up and saw it leave through her exhalation as her facial expression relaxed back to neutral.

Finally, her guard was coming down.

"Jazmin, don't talk. Just listen." I said, still gently massaging her thighs. She looked at me in agreement without saying anything.

"I know this is a little much for one night. Me, with all this drama about getting cheated on. But I need you. I have a lot going on and I just don't feel like thinking about any of it. Instead, I'd rather act on what I'm feeling right now, and that's an unbelievable amount of physical attraction for you. I ran out on you before, but it just kinda caught me off guard and I wasn't ready. Doesn't mean I didn't want you. Sometimes we feel things that don't make sense to us, but the only way to know for sure what it means is to do something about it. I don't want to compromise our friendship, but I lost control over that a long time ago. At this point, I think it's time we both figure out what it is that's drawing us to one another. Something brought you to try and kiss me before, and something's bringing me to try and do the same thing right now. If you want to know exactly what that something is, then don't stop me."

I continued to massage her thigh as I leaned in closer to her face for a kiss. For every inch closer I went, I anticipated a hand on my chest pushing me backwards. But it didn't happen. She didn't stop me, or even try to move out of the way.

She began closing her eyes when I got close enough, so I did the same, softly pecking her on the lips.

I pecked her again and again, each time easing my tongue onto hers.

She kissed me back, and I slid my hand up to her vagina, met with what seemed like the Pacific Ocean. Then I stopped and stood up from the bed.

She snapped, "What are you doing? Why you stop? Shawn don't play games with me. This is not the time to start with your fucking games!" She was getting angry at what she thought was me getting ready to bail on her again.

I just looked at her, in slight amazement of how I had drawn her into the moment so much, and aroused by the control I now had.

I took off my shirt and unfastened my belt.

She looked me up and down, anxiously waiting to read just how excited I was by the extent of my erection.

Then, a memory of Danielle flashed across my mind. It had been so long since I was doing this with another woman, and I didn't like the feeling it was giving, but I needed it more than anything for refuge from the onslaught of truth about my love life being in shambles.

It was the only thing thus far that actually distracted me from those images of her with Lewis, and the imagination of what else was happening when I wasn't around.

I felt my erection failing me the longer I dwelled on those thoughts, so I cut the nightstand lamp off to try and hide it. Took her hand and placed it on my stomach to revive me.

She felt around on my stomach a bit, and immediately, I was back to full strength.

I almost forgot the feeling of wondering whether or not I was going to receive oral sex. It was unpredictable.

It was exciting.

The way that she bit her bottom lip at the touch of my penis told me she was just as excited as I was.

She put her forehead to my stomach, and I could feel myself in her mouth. Her tongue was doing a figure 8 number on the tip of me as she sucked, something I know I didn't teach her, but was grateful to whoever gave her the lesson.

She was amazing. I'm not sure if she was just trying to impress me, but if so, it worked.

I pulled back so I wouldn't come too fast once we actually started having sex. Went back to kiss her again, this time reaching around her and unhooking her bra.

"Shawn, do you have something to put on it?" she said.

I looked around trying to see what she was talking about, then saw her looking at my penis and back up at me.

"Something like what? What you mean?"

"What you mean, *what I mean*? I mean a condom. I'm not on the pill and I don't need none of your jr.'s running 'round here. You need to put on a condom."

I forgot all about using protection during sex. I had been with Danielle for over three years now and we hadn't used any since we made it official. During the moment it took to realize why I didn't have a condom, my thoughts came back about the luxury of trust I no longer had with my partner.

She saw me staring blankly and said, "You don't have one, do you?" Then she got up and walked over to her closet. She reached up on the top shelf and pulled down an old shoe box.

I could tell it was something she hadn't been in for a while with how clumsily she was searching through it. But then she picked something out and dropped the box where she was standing.

"Here, put this on. I know it's not as big as you might need, but it's all I got."

"Uh, yeah. Okay cool," I said, nervously trying to remember how to put on a condom. Trying to figure out which way it rolled in the dark was like shooting a three-pointer on a moving rim. The lubrication made it too slippery and I was feeling the pressure from her waiting that I normally didn't have to worry about.

Finally I just forced it on. It wasn't pretty, but it was going to have to do.

She lay back on the bed, inviting me between her thighs. By this time, the streetlights were shining through just enough that I could make out general details of her frame.

It was just as sexy as I had imagined when I saw her in the house walking around in her underwear.

Then, this weird feeling came over me. It was cold, and even in her presence, very alone. Started thinking about the times Danielle and I would be in the same position.

But this was different because I was hurting, and on the run from something that I could never get away from; the truth.

Jasmine was saying something to me, but I was already gone. I could feel the tears filling up my eyes as I was reminded of the intimate moments Danielle had been sharing with another man.

She had broken my heart, yet every single fragment still belonged to her.

"Shawn. Shawn. SHAWN!" Jazmin said, interrupting my daze.

"Huh?"

"Why are you just sitting there? See, look what you've done, you let it go soft." I looked down and saw my penis cowering in what looked like a wet trash bag around it. "You know what, how about you just lie down," she said, getting off the bed again.

I moved to the other side. She grabbed me, then tried to swallow me whole.

After a few seconds, she took off the mangled condom, threw it on the dresser, and continued to suck. I started coming back to life again.

I closed my eyes and tried to block out my thoughts. I was here now, and I needed to finish what I started.

It wasn't like Danielle and I had some kind of commitment to each other anymore. Clearly she had moved on. I needed to do the same. My conscience was still in a relationship, but I wasn't sure if I was.

Jazmin was amazing at oral sex. She could have given a workshop on some of the things she was doing. The movements, the sounds, the breathing, and everything else about her, was as good as I had ever experienced with any woman.

I was finally loosening up again and relaxing until I felt something different.

It was much warmer.

And wetter.

I opened my eyes and looked up to see Jazmin on top of me, and me inside of her.

Shit. What was I doing?

I knew better than this, but she did it so fast and fluently I couldn't even tell she had transitioned her entire body weight until it was already done.

But it was too late. Couldn't stop now, especially with me being the one bringing the whole situation into fruition in the first place. Anything I could catch was already caught, and I didn't feel like going through the whole condom thing again. It was no turning back, I could only hope *pulling out* worked.

Trying to convince myself to believe in that rationale was taking so much effort, I had become numb. Again.

Jazmin was yelling and moaning loudly, so I assumed she was enjoying herself. But other than that, my feeling was gone, this time throughout my entire body.

Everything went into slow motion, and it was then that I realized exactly what I had set out to learn in the beginning. The answer to the question of exactly what that 'something' was that was drawing me to Jazmin.

I lost focus and ultimately appreciation for the things I had because of my distraction turned curiosity for the things I didn't have. A man could have a million dollars, but if he only focused on the penny on the ground, he would lose sight of his fortune, giving someone else the opportunity to take it from him.

My fortune was being taken and I wanted it back.

I felt Jazmin's body shiver violently and her moans got louder. She did this back in the day when she climaxed, so I knew exactly what it meant.

"Did you come?" I asked her.

"Yeah I did, but only twice. I want one more."

"I'm about to come, though," I lied. I wasn't anywhere near an orgasm. I just needed to get things over with as smoothly as possible. My mind was no longer on sex.

"Oh okay, you need me to get up right now or can you go a little longer?"

"Right now." I grabbed her by her waist and picked her up off of me.

She was probably going to be looking for the semen somewhere so I ran into the bathroom and closed the door. Never did this when I pulled out, normally it would just end up wherever I aimed it, but then again, I never faked an orgasm either.

I let a few seconds go by then flushed the toilet. My penis, still erect, was being stubborn. I leaned over the sink and ran cold water over it to make it go back to sleep.

It was time for me to come up with an escape plan that was going to allow me to save face.

I opened the door and saw her sprawled out on the bed. She was still panting, but her body was motionless.

"Babe, that was great," she said, with her eyes half open fixed on the ceiling. "I'm gon' cook you a nice breakfast in the morning. You earned it."

Babe? She was already moving too fast. Staying over for breakfast? She had me mixed up. I felt my "ain't shit" instincts coming back from freshman year preparing me to hurt her feelings.

I walked back over and stood at the foot of the bed. "Um, yeah, it was good for me too. But I think I'mma go on back home. I don't have anything over here to sleep in and I might be late to class if I try to get all of that done in the morning."

She sat up in the bed and glared at me. "So what, you just gon' fuck me and then just leave? Is that what I am to you? Some kind of two dollar whore?"

I wanted to tell her that actually a two dollar whore would be more expensive because she was free, but it was no time for humor. "No Jaz, you know it's not like that at all. I do want to stay. I just need something to put on and I know you don't have-"

"I still have some of Lewis' old clothes if you wanna wear those."

I all but blew the fuck up. "No! And don't bring his name up to me again. You hear me?!" I yelled.

She looked at me surprised and confused. "All right, damn. I won't do it again."

I caught myself. I had thought that having sex with his ex-girlfriend would do something for me, but it didn't. His name felt like a knife in my side.

Now I was beginning to feel like a complete jerk for not only trying to hit it and leave, but then yelling at her.

I looked at her again and could see I had hurt her feelings.

From the very beginning, she was only trying to help. She trusted me, exactly as I asked her to.

I needed to honor that and at minimum, not make her feel like shit by leaving in the middle of the night after faking an orgasm. Besides, it was still a little too soon to see Danielle. The dust was probably never going to completely settle, but it was a huge gamble to go back on the same night.

"Move over and give me some covers. If I'mma sleep naked, I gotta make sure I'm warm enough so I don't catch a cold."

Her face relaxed into a slight grin as she made room next to her in the bed. "I knew you wasn't about to leave. At least, I wasn't about to let you." She tried to cuddle up next to me so I lay flat on my stomach so she couldn't. That move was reserved for my fortune, not the penny.

"Wake, up boo. I told you I'd cook for you and I don't want you blaming me for being late either. Come on, wake up."

I opened my eyes to see Jazmin standing over me with a tray of food and orange juice. She was wearing my t-shirt from last night and smiling from ear to ear. This had gone too far a long time ago. It was time for a talk.

"Thanks, you can set it over there for right now. But real quick, Jaz, I wanna talk to you."

"Yes?" she said, still smiling. I hated that what I was about to say was going to make her do everything but smile, but it needed to be said.

"Jaz, you're my best friend, and I appreciate everything you've done for me. Really, I do. But I think I made up my mind about what I wanna do about with my situation. You may or may not like it but I hope you understand."

She stopped smiling and it made it hard to keep eye contact. But I kept going.

"You and I...we need to just fall back from each other. I mean you haven't done anything wrong or nothin'. I just feel like I'm a mess and I've invited you into it to make it even worse. I've been selfish, only thinkin' about myself. Never should have drug you into this."

"So you say all this now, after we've had sex, after everything we've been through and you tell me this now?"

"I know. I know. I just, I have to figure this out on my own. And I don't need to open any doors until every other one is closed. You're an amazing person. Really, you are. But the amount of me I'm able to give you is way less than you deserve. I'd be doing you a disservice by even trying when I know where my heart is at. I couldn't have asked for a better friend, but if I don't end this now, then I never was your friend to begin with."

She stared at me expressionless. Then I saw a tear drop from her left eye and it made my heart sink. It really sucked to know I was hurting her. But I had to.

"Shawn, you can't just expect me to be cool with this. Sex isn't just sex to me anymore. My body is special, and if I share that with you, it's because I think you're special. I've been looking, all my life, for a reason to feel that way and meeting you was proof that I was worth the try. Things didn't work out with Lewis, but talking with you helped me see that there's some good guys out here who think more of me than just a good fuck and cool conversation. But in the same way you're not being selfish, I don't wanna be selfish either. If you need to cut things off with me, then that's just what you need to do. It hurts like hell, but I support you," she said, wiping the tears from her face.

I didn't expect the emotional response she gave. More like a pot of grits splashing on me which actually would have been better.

I couldn't blame her for anything she felt. She was entitled to it all. But even if I couldn't make things right, I at least kept things from getting worse.

"Thank you. Take care," I said. Wasn't sure if that was the last words I'd ever say to her, but if it was, it summed up our friendship and the way I wanted to end.

She took my shirt off then handed it to me and went into the bathroom to, I believe, change clothes. I didn't wait to find out.

Instead, I slipped on my pants, and headed out the door with the rest in hand. I got in my car and started it up and remembered my phone was kept off the charger all night so it had to be dead by now.

I plugged it up to the charger and saw it light up with a line of missed calls from Danielle.

She had been calling from 1 a.m. all the way until 5 a.m., nonstop, every 10 minutes.

Maybe she saw me pull off last night after all.

I started to call her back but hesitated because I didn't know what to say. I could go off about what I saw, or I could wait and see if she would just come out and confess.

That would mean she at least felt some kind of regret about cheating, and it'd help me learn to trust her again. Even though I had realized how much she meant to me, I still had to learn to deal with the fact that she was seeing another guy. It was too many thoughts to deal with so I just drove back home getting ready to cross that bridge when I got to it.

I pulled up and saw her car still in the same place, this time with my parking spot empty. I was barefoot and shirtless, and if I was trying to be obvious, I'm pretty sure that could do the trick.

I started putting my clothes back on. Even though I had every right to tell her what I had done without her getting mad, I still felt uncomfortable with the idea. Something just didn't seem right about it, but maybe I just needed to be face to face with her before it made sense.

I walked in and saw all the lights on in the house, apparently from the night before because it was still early. Danielle was sitting on the couch, still in the same clothes she wore yesterday, but leaning on the arm rest asleep.

She never went to sleep leaving the lights on.

"Danielle, Danielle," I whispered, seeing if she'd wake up. She was out cold. Calling me till five o'clock in the morning had worn her out. I tapped her shoulder. "Danielle, get up. Why you got all these lights burning?"

"Huh? Superman, that you?" she said, still waking up. Her morning voice was so innocent and almost childlike. It used to make me hold her tighter when we first woke up and she'd tell me she loved me.

"Yeah, it's me. You need to get up and get in the bed. You got all these lights on."

"I was waiting for you. Where have you been? I was trying to call you all night, I thought something had happened. I didn't know what to do." Her voice was still a little scratchy but she was coming to.

"I had to get away for a minute, had some things I had to get off my mind. I would have answered but I didn't hear my phone ringing."

"Oh, well, I'm glad you're all right. Are you hungry? I'm sorry I didn't cook yet, I would have but I fell asleep."

"No, I'm not hungry, but I do have a question. What were you doing last night? And please, just be honest," I said looking her in the eye. I knew she didn't expect me to ask her at the moment but that made it even better of a time to finally bring it up. I needed to know and I needed to know right then.

"What do you mean, be honest? What are you talking about? I was here."

"Here with who, Danielle? Don't play dumb."

She sat up and looked at me still squinting but wide awake now. "I'm not playing dumb. I was here, I promise. I didn't go anywhere all night."

"Danielle, I just want you to tell me the truth. I'm not saying I won't be mad, but I need you to come out and be real about whatever it is you were doing."

"I am being real. I don't have anything to lie about. Why don't you just say what you're trying to say already instead of talking crazy like I did something wrong."

"Okay, well, since you wanna play it like that, cool. I saw you. I saw you last night. You and Lewis were up in here while I was gone. You didn't think I saw you, but I saw both of y'all hugged up at the door and everything."

She looked away and shook her head. That was all the confirmation I needed right there. I knew it.

Then she started laughing.

I said, "What's so funny?"

"You."

"What you mean me? I don't think this is funny and it's messed up that you think it's a joke."

"Well, it is funny. I mean, yeah I had him in here, but it wasn't like I was sleeping with him or anything. I had him here because he needed my book to do last minute studying. Normally he asks me to send my notes but instead of me telling him no I just told him he can come get the book and do the work for himself. So he did. I know it was late and all but he called my bluff. The least I could do was actually help him. He wasn't here for a real long time, just like 10 minutes or so for an overview and then he left. And I wasn't hugged up with him, I just gave him a hug, that's it. I don't know why you're being all over dramatic, you should have just asked instead of assuming. I can't believe you think I'd do something like that. He's not even my type. Ugh." She got up and walked back into the bedroom.

My chest started pounding and I took the seat she had just vacated. This news should have been a relief, but it was devastating.

It would've been better if she had a confession, even a mild one. Maybe that she had been getting to know him for a while but it never went past that, or that she wanted to cheat one time but couldn't do it and was sending him on his way, anything but this.

Now I was left shit-faced. Guilt was bum-rushing me, and weight that few people could lift on their own had placed itself on my shoulders. I couldn't say a word.

I should have went and apologized before even accusing her. Then again, what's an apology without a promise to do better? What's a promise with a track record of infidelity? I lost all respect from and for myself.

When It All Falls Down

After a few minutes, she came and kissed me on her way out the door. She seemed to have brushed off the conversation from earlier, while I was stuck thinking of absolutely nothing else.

We don't realize what our choices could mean for us until after they're made. I lost my only friend, and now on the brink of losing the love of my life, and I did it with one stupid choice. Now all that was left was the decision to either tell her the truth.

Or hide it from her.

If I told her, she was not only going to leave me, but she was bound to be heartbroken. Could I really handle that?

I know I didn't want to find out. I mean, it was already done. There was no amount of will power to re-do it, or amount of sincere apology that could go back in time and make the right choice.

When you break someone's heart, you break their sanity and she didn't deserve that at all. I did. All the times I told her and showed her I loved her would mean absolutely nothing. As for now, her heart and sanity were still intact. The only thing that could change that was her finding out the truth.

So in a way, there was a positive left to be had and that's that the damage of my decision was still internal and mine to suffer.

This catastrophe didn't have to happen to anyone else but me, if I could only conceal it well enough and maybe even long enough for it to just go away. If it didn't go away, then... I guess I'd take it to the grave. But I damn sure couldn't bring myself to even imagine what it'd be like to let those words leave my mouth; that I did the very thing I vowed against since the first day we admitted our love to one another.

Honestly, I didn't mean to. I mean I meant to, but...damn. I was wrong. But I was in too deep. So, that was it, I just wasn't going to tell her and she wasn't going to find out.

Even though we were no longer friends, I knew Jazmin wouldn't say anything about it.

We didn't end on bad terms so she had no reason to be spiteful and I definitely wasn't going to go back and have sex with her or any girl again for that matter. I learned my lesson. I hated even entertaining the thought of keeping something this significant from my woman, but I wasn't prepared for this. Not one bit.

I went to class that day feeling like I was walking knee high in mud. I could have pushed a car up a hill with the effort it took just to get from one place to another. I didn't feel good about myself; I couldn't be nice to anyone; and I was stressed out the entire day. This cheating thing looked a lot easier when Stevie J did it.

I looked at my phone and saw Danielle's text.

Meet me in the cafe at 1:30. My class got cancelled n I wanna eat lunch w/u

Great. I needed everything but to be around her with the pressure I was already taking from my conscience. But she was up all night waiting for me to get home, the least I could do is sit with her and eat lunch.

It was exactly 1:15 and my class still wasn't dismissed. I grabbed my bag and excused myself so I could be there on the time. Not a lot of room for error.

I walked in the cafeteria scanning the tables for her. Didn't look like she had made it in yet, so I went and picked us a spot off in the corner and set my books down. I looked down to text her so she'd know I had made it in and then I felt a hand on my shoulder. I damn near hopped out my seat.

"Whoa, calm down. I just wanted to give you your watch. You left it on my nightstand, I thought you might need it."

"Jazmin? How'd you know I'd be in here?" My heart was thumping and I felt my pores open like flood gates for the sweat that was now beading up on my nose.

"Chill out. I ain't know you was gon' be nowhere. I was getting ready to leave and was holding onto in case I saw you today. Here, take it. I'm gone now. Bye," she said, putting my watch on the table and walking off. This was all too damn coincidental for me. I needed a cup of water and some deodorant. Fast.

I looked at the watch and saw it said 1:34. I walked over to the buffet table to pick out some lunch that I now had absolutely no appetite for and caught a glimpse of Danielle coming through the door. I played it cool like I didn't see her, for no particular reason, just seemed like a smart thing to do.

"Hey, Superman."

"Hey, baby, 'bout time you made it in. I been waiting for like 30 minutes."

"Oh whatever, I'm only five minutes late. You probably just got here yourself."

Laughing I said, "Yeah I did. I got us a seat over there in the corner. If you want, I'll fix ya plate and you can go head and sit down. I'll bring it to you."

She didn't hesitate to take me up on the offer. She looked damn good. Her jeans were fitting right, and she had just under too much cleavage showing, how I liked it.

However, this wasn't the day to admire that. I had to use every moment I could to make sure I calculated my next move. I had maintained a pretty good poker face so far.

I just had to keep it up and let time work its magic on the rest. I finally started believing the 'it's gon' be okay' line I had been telling myself all day.

I finished loading up the plates with lunch selects: fried chicken and watermelon that I wouldn't dare think about eating in front of white people, some mixed veggies, and rice. Came back to the table to see her face buried in a book, seemingly looking over some notes from one of her classes.

"What you got there?"

"Some stuff from my history class. Can you believe that? History. We're in college, and still required to take a damn history class," she said without looking up. She was good for talking without making eye contact.

"Well, it's good that you're well-rounded. I mean, you know what they say about history. Those who don't know it are forced to repeat it."

"Oh, if I don't know this history, I'll damn sure repeat it."

"Don't think like that."

"Well, I don't see what the Bear River massacre has to do with my sales and marketing degree. Unless I'm marketing to Indians, then I guess it could come in handy."

"Baby, don't trip. You know college isn't really meant to teach you much. It's just supposed to test you, give employers a weeding-out process, and see if you have the chops to make it through some shit you know is unnecessarily difficult."

"And loan debt. Don't forget that part. Sallie Mae's the biggest pimp the world's ever seen. I know when I graduate she's going to have her powder ready to slap me with those high interest rates."

"Well, that's what a job is for. Better to be paying off loans in a house rather than living under a bridge debt-free. You picked your poison, and I think it's a good one."

"Ugh. I don't wanna do this right now." She snapped her book close and pushed it to the side. I was already halfway done with my food.

"Everything okay?"

"Yeah, it's cool. I just, I don't know. My nerves are bad right now," she said, rubbing her temples.

I got up and went around the table to massage her shoulders. She loved my massages and I loved that she loved them. It always gave me a proud feeling when I could take things off her mind.

"Superman?"

"Yes, sweetheart?"

"Why you being so nice to me? Is it because you don't want me to be mad at you for accusing me of cheating? 'Cause just so you know, I ain't forgot."

My throat closed up. It felt like I was trying to swallow a medicine ball. I was all for keeping the subject off of this and sticking to talking about how college is just another part of the system.

"What you mean? Ain't I supposed to be nice to you? Yeah, I was out of line earlier but that was earlier. This is now. I just want to make you feel a lil' better, that's all."

I could sense her rolling her eyes while I kept massaging her shoulders. "Mmmhm. Yeah okay, don't be tryna butter me up now." I reached down and kissed her on the cheek. She and I both knew she loved it when I did stuff like that in public. Public display of affection to a woman is like floor seats at the NBA finals for a man. Okay, maybe not that good, but pretty close.

I felt hopeful the rest of the day. I got to a point where I was treating the memories of the night before like a bad dream. Something I didn't want to think about, and hopefully would forget about later.

But it was still taking a distracting amount of effort to keep putting it to the back burner of my mind. People underestimate the energy it takes to think. I felt like I was about to pull a muscle in my brain any moment at the rate I was going.

After my last class I went down to the weight room. Football season was over with and since it was my last year, I had started prepping for pro day. I had perfect weight and height, and with my strength, I was on course to break the all-time record for the bench press. My footwork was my weakest area and I had been going down to do one-on-one training with my conditioning coach to fix it. Ladder drills, step- ups, box jumps, parachute sprints, we did it all. About three hour's worth.

I finished up and I looked at my phone. No missed calls. No texts. That was different. Got in my car and headed home.

Sex with Jazmin was on my mind. I needed to go get tested. I never should have gone inside her raw. Hands down, the dumbest decision I ever made.

I wanted to talk to Danielle about it so bad. We could always vent to each other about what was on our minds. But not this time. It felt unnatural. Like she was a stranger I couldn't trust, but really it was me. I was the stranger. Definitely not who she thought I was. The guilt was eating at me, leaving me empty.

I pulled up to the apartment not long after dark and saw her car there but the lights were off. Probably in the room studying like she always was. Worked for me. The less talking we did, the better chance I had of not saying the wrong thing.

I walked in and thought I picked the wrong door. There were candles everywhere, off-white balloons, some champagne, and two silver platters on the living room table. I could hear Keith Sweat playing faintly from somewhere in the bedroom. Danielle was on the couch with a wine glass in her hand.

"Baby? What's all of this?"

"I thought you'd never get here. I've been waiting on you," she said, walking up to me and handing me the cup. "I hope you're hungry. I cooked. And no, it's not spaghetti."

"You did all this? Danielle....wow....what's the occasion?" I couldn't help but be suspicious. This was unlike her. I didn't know if she was planning on this being my last meal or what because she was hardly the romantic type.

"You're the occasion, Superman. I thought it was about time I did something nice for you. Show you a little more attention. Clearly I'm doing something wrong if you think I'm out here running around on you. So instead of getting mad, I realized that I need to do more to assure you that I am all...yours..."she said wrapping her arms around my neck and kissing me through the end of the sentence.

My heart sunk down into my socks. I couldn't believe what was happening to me. All this time I had been waiting for this day, and now that it was here, I could all but enjoy it. I closed my eyes and hugged her as I lost the fight against uncontrollable tears demanding to be let out.

We were still embraced, but when I didn't say anything back to her, she began loosening her grip to try and see my face.

"Shawn, what's...what's the matter? You don't like it?" she said, now looking at me worried.

I lost it. I started crying uncontrollably. The guilt mixed with the beauty of the woman that was before me was far too much to keep my composure.

I had no right to keep this from her any longer. At first it seemed like a great idea. Like my only option. But even if I could pull it off without her ever finding out, there's no way I could look myself in the mirror knowing that everything from that point forward would be based on a lie. The lie that I was as committed to her as she was to me.

Whether or not I was going to hurt her with my truth was irrelevant. The fact that I made the truth hurtful was what really mattered. I couldn't just rob her of the right to know what really happened. The other way around, I know I wouldn't want to know. But more so, I wouldn't want to be with anyone who had the moral fiber or lack thereof to keep it from me.

This sucked. But I had to do something about it.

"Superman, you're scaring me. Tell me what's wrong with you. Please."

"Danielle...sit down. We need to talk."

She grabbed me by the hand and led me to the couch.

Nurturing.

She was always so nurturing.

I was going to miss that.

"Before I start, I need to make something clear."

"Okay."

"I love you."

"I love you too."

"Don't say it back, Danielle." she looked at me stunned and surprised at what I said.

"Why can't I say it back? I do love you."

"Because you might not feel that way after I tell you what I have to tell you." A tension came in the room so thick you could throw a dart into it and it'd stick. Fear was written all over her face. Fear of what she already knew I was about to tell her. But that wasn't enough, I had to finish.

"I never meant to hurt you." Tears started filling my eyes again. I damn near couldn't breathe. "I cheated. I cheated and I'm so sorry."

She didn't move or make any change in her face. She continued to look at me as her tears and mine began to mirror each other. We sat there a few seconds.

"But why?"

"I don't have a reason, and there's definitely no excuse. Not one that's valid. I'm so sorry."

"When?" she said coldly.

I sat there and looked at her. By the way she looked back at me I could see that she knew exactly when.

"So you mean to tell me, that all this time I was up worried about you, you were out sleeping with some other *bitch?"*

I tried to speak a few times and was successful on one of my tries. "Yes. And I was wrong. I'm so sorry."

"Don't give me that sorry shit." she said getting up and walking in the bedroom. I heard her snatch the cord of the radio from the wall. She flipped the lights on again and the mood changed instantly. She had gotten pretty hot with me before, but this time she was nuclear.

"How could you? You told me you'd never do this. You said you were different."

"Danielle, I'm...I'm sorry."

"That means about as much as the rest of that bullshit you been feeding me. I'm so disgusted I can't even look at you right now. You're no better than these other niggas. You got some nerve and then come right up in here acting like everything's okay."

"I can't blame you for being mad, but I promise, I didn't mean to hurt you. I don't wanna come off like I'm tryna justify what I did because it was foul, but you have to know that I love you and I'm sorry."

"You know what, if you say you sorry one more time I swear."

"I know you're mad. You have every right to be. If I could do it over again I would. I mean I'd do it differently. I wouldn't have been so stupid as to have let one night ruin everything we've built over the years."

"Oh, you were stupid all right."

"I would've come home, and stayed home. But I didn't. I can't go back and do it again. All I can say is that I'm sorry and if you give me a chance, I'll make it more than words. I'll show you that I do love you. Because I do."

"I know you're sorry. A sorry piece of-"

"I can see why you'd say that but I have to-"

"Just...stop it. You've done enough talking. Now let me speak. I have never...*ever* trusted someone with my heart like I have you. I've never invested myself into someone like I have you. I've never loved anyone like you. If I could take it all back, I would. A man says what he means and means exactly what he says. You can't look me in my eye and tell me you love me then go out and sleep around. Actions speak louder than words and nothing about yours say a word about you being a man. You're a piece of shit just like the sperm donor that left you. Clearly the apple doesn't fall far from the tree."

Her words struck like lightning. Lightning I deserved to feel. She had a way of reaching to depths of me no one else could possibly reach to get her point across.

"This is all my fault and I accept full responsibility for my actions. I don't know another way to apologize but I did do the best I could in at least telling you the truth."

"You didn't mess up, you *are* messed up. You're a mess all together. You don't do shit right. And you jump at any piece of ass that's thrown your way. Oh and don't try that 'I at least told you the truth' shit because that doesn't make it right. You're still as no good as the rest of these niggas and I hope your daughter grows up to marry one so she can feel just how you're making me feel right now." I had never heard her talk like this. Ever.

"Okay Danielle. I got it. I'll get my stuff and I'll go."

"No, you stay, I'll go. I don't want to be in this house any longer. I don't want to be reminded of all the shit I did for you tonight to try and show your cheating ass some special attention. I just want you to know that you really had something good going in your life, for once. And you just ruined it. No, as a matter of fact, you didn't ruin it. You cheated on it, but it will be just fine without your *sorry* ass. I can promise you that."

She went back into the room and stuffed random clothes into a duffle bag. As much as I didn't want to be selfish, what she had just said was now overpowering the freedom I was supposed to have from telling the truth.

They say that when you're mad you say things you don't mean. I believe that when you're mad, you say things you've been meaning to say but never did. But is that what she really thought of me? It was no time to ask, nor care.

This was just as bad as I thought it'd be and I didn't see it getting much better any time soon. The end of that night couldn't come soon enough.

Flawed Hearts Break Too

I woke up on the couch, smelling the scent of candles burned down to the wax and stale food. I didn't remember falling asleep nor was I sure what time I fell asleep.

Danielle was gone, definitely, but other than that, I wasn't sure of much of anything. Shit just didn't feel right. I didn't know what it was that I wanted. I just knew I didn't have it.

Tired of crying and exhausted from trying to decide what in the hell to do with my life, I closed my eyes and lay back down on the couch.

Danielle's last words were sharp, and she shoved them as deeply into my stomach as she could.

You're a piece of shit just like the sperm donor that left you. She really didn't have to go there. Even out of anger, there's just some things you don't say, but I guess there's some things you just don't do also, like cheat.

You still as no good as the rest of these niggas and I hope your daughter grows up to marry one. Clearly she wouldn't wish that on her own child. So plans of us having a family were out the window.

As a matter of fact, you didn't ruin it. You cheated on it, but it will be just fine without your sorry ass. Yeah, if there ever was an end, this was it. I was afraid of hurting her and ultimately breaking her, but I was wrong. She'd be just fine without my sorry ass. As she should be.

She knew the truth, I gave it my best shot at breaking it to her easy, and we didn't have to call the cops. For some reason it still didn't feel like I did enough. I just felt hollow.

I broke her heart and mine in the same moment. Some champ I was.

I needed somebody to talk to. Maybe someone who could tell me it was going to be okay. Somebody who could pretend to care, so I could pretend to believe them, so we could both pretend I wasn't the jerk I knew I was.

That was wishful thinking at its best. Realistically, they'd say, "You know it's your fault. I hope you learned your lesson." Or "You did the right thing, now you know better for next time." Hell, I didn't want a next time if at any point it could possibly feel like this. And what did their opinions matter anyway? Everyone acts like you deserve any punishment you get for whatever crime you commit, so long as they're not the ones committing it.

It was then that I realized that growing up was an evil process. Inevitably hard lessons to learn, a world full of people ready to crack the whip when you learned them, and pain being the one thing that'll be there for you at the end of it all.

I counted every blessing I had, and it never added up to losing the best thing that ever happened to me. I think they call that depression. A deep hole you can't climb out of that only gets deeper the longer you fall.

I didn't trust anyone to be able to pull me out, and even if they could, they probably wouldn't. I was too exhausted to keep lying, and my truth was only going to justify the boot in my face they'd give me to make me fall faster once I reminded them of someone they hated.

I didn't fit into this world. No matter how I compared myself to people, I wasn't one of the good ones.

I hurt those who were loyal to me, and I wasn't completely sure I'd never do it again if given another chance. Not because I didn't want to, but because of my ability to be human, and people's inability to understand.

They would only give me lessons they never learned about loyalty. That's what got me in this mess. Loyalty. It's the very opposite of its definition because there's no way you can be loyal to one without being disloyal to everyone else. There'll come a point when more than one person will need you at the same time. And when you choose, no matter how you do so, you will lose at least one of them.

Life was teaching me what no one else could. And what it was teaching me, was making me hate it. It didn't have to go like this. I was born without this knowledge, and receiving it shouldn't have to hurt this badly.

Yet and still, Danielle was my main concern. She didn't deserve for me to happen to her, and I hate that I did. There's nothing I could possibly do to turn back the hands of time to fix things, but there was one thing I could do to stop the hands of time from breaking things again.

I started praying.

"Dear God, if you can hear me, I need you. Thanking you for any blessings with my words would be a slap in the face with what my actions are doing to show my lack of appreciation, so I'll spare you. I'm not here calling on you because we're best friends. We both know that's not the truth. But I'm here because I need a blessing I don't deserve. Probably not the first time you've heard that. You give blessings to people who don't deserve 'em all the time. You bless deadbeat dads with beautiful children. You bless people who scheme all their lives with their dream house and cars. You bless liars with the ability to run for political offices and make laws that are only in their own interest. But I'm not asking for any of those things. Lord I'm asking for peace. Peace in knowing that Danielle will get the happiness she deserves even without me, peace in knowing that you and I can somehow get back to how we used to be. God, I just want peace. You don't have to say anything back, but please answer my prayer. I don't have anyone else. Amen."

I opened my eyes again to feel tears dropping like rain, then wiped them so I could make out the floor well enough to watch my step on my way out of the house.

I grabbed a hold of the railing going down the stairs to the parking lot, forgetting how I had not eaten in almost 24 hours. I was weak, shaking, and had a throbbing headache. Something needed to happen. I just wanted all this to stop

I popped open the trunk of my car, moved some old cleats out of the way, and there it was. My answer to not only my problems, but also every woman's problem that I would have otherwise encountered in the future.

The gun I was trying to give Jazmin was still tucked safely in the back of the trunk and the one courtesy bullet was there too. I was always scared of what it could be like to welcome death, but with all that life was doing to me at the moment, there wasn't much lower I could go, and upwards wasn't looking too hopeful either.

This was less about me, but more so about the sacrifice I needed to make in order to save everyone from me. The only two people that cared about me were in pain, and it was my fault. I was in pain, and it was my fault. Everything was my fault, and for once I needed to keep a promise, a promise to stop hurting people.

I closed the trunk and went back upstairs. My eyes were still burning and my stomach was growling with no remorse.

I went into the bedroom, then into the closet, and it looked like a tornado hit it from the night before when Danielle went through it for her belongings. Clothes were everywhere, some hanging halfway off the hanger, most on the floor.

We always had a keepsake box that we said we'd show our children of what it was like when we were their age one day. Last I remember, it was in the closet but with my body aching for more sleep and breakfast, it was getting tough to find it.

I slung the clothes out into the bedroom, trying to let the carpet breathe for a better chance of finding it, and sure enough I saw it emerge from the very back on the right side with all the other stuff we hadn't touched in ages.

I sat down and opened it up to the strong scent of Danielle from about a year and a half ago when I bought her the new Beyonce fragrance for Christmas. That was when she suggested we make a memory box together.

My old high school football newspaper articles, a few old pencils, but mostly printouts from cell phone pictures we took on our first few dates were in there. I got a bit choked up as I was reminded of all the good times we had.

One picture was from our first movie date when I spent my last dime on tickets and her meal and had to pretend I wasn't hungry while I watched her eat. I was your average broke college student aiming for an above average girl so I did what I had to do. It was worth it, and I don't think she knew just how broke I went trying to be a gentleman.

Another picture was from the first time I took her to the fair. She asked me for a piggy back ride, and even though I was sore from football practice, I accepted. After a few miles of walking, my legs were locking up and burning all up and down my hamstrings. Out of sheer pride, I kept walking so she wouldn't think she was too heavy. That was my baby.

I grabbed the pictures from the box and stood back up into reality. I was alone again, cold, and while not heartless, the one I had didn't work.

I didn't know much about suicides, I guess not many people get a chance to practice, but I did know that they usually come with a note. Looking over to the corner of the room I spotted one of my notebooks, the paper in it barely touched. Not sure of what to say, but this would all be for nothing if it was misunderstood.

I couldn't always articulate verbally what I felt, but writing was something that allowed me to be more transparent. I grabbed the notebook and a pencil nearby and started writing:

To all those it may concern:

I just want to say I'm sorry. If I ever hurt you, if I ever lied to you, if I ever did you wrong, I'm sorry. I don't know if there's a way to make amends for something you can't take back, but if actions speak louder than words, then I hope you hear my next one for the rest of your life that I truly mean this apology. I don't blame anyone but me, and I take full accountability.

<u>Momma</u>: You were the best mother anyone could ask for. You showed me so much and I'm so glad God gave you to me because he didn't have to. I don't have a lot of money left, but what's in my account is yours to help with the funeral costs. I'll be watching over you until we meet again. Love you, Momma.

<u>My sisters</u>: Since I was born, you all looked out for me, and I can't thank you enough. I'm sorry for not being someone

you could be proud of, but I never took for granted the things you taught me about life. Tell my nieces and nephews, once they're old enough to understand, that their uncle loved them dearly and they can do anything they set their minds to. Kiss them for me often. Love y'all.

My Dad: We never got to know each other, and now we never will. I think you would've been proud of me for the most part, but I needed you in ways you'll never understand. At the end of the day, I'm doing what I have to do, the way a man should. Love you, Dad.

Danielle: I don't know what else to say, but I love you. I didn't show it very well, I know. And I know you probably don't believe me...but it's true. I hope you can learn to forgive me, not for me, but for you. You deserve the peace of mind it'll take to move on and find a man who's never going to hurt you. You're special in so many ways and 'amazing' is an understatement to describe you, but it's the closest I have to sum you up in one word. I made a mistake I can't undo and life isn't life without you so this is my goodbye. You'll never have to see me again, at least until God reunites us, this time without my flaws, and ready to love you the way I should have before. I promised to protect you no matter what, and I will keep that promise. I should have done it the day we met, and just walked away until I was ready, but instead I took a chance...and I failed. But I won't fail again.

If I didn't mention you, please forgive me. I can't see very well because of my tears but trust me, I haven't forgotten you. But it's time for me to go now.

Sincerely,

Shawn

I left the letter lying on the dining room table in between the two silver platters of food from the night before. Pretty sure that'd be an easy place to find it, and it was as good as it was going to get without a bulletin board.

I grabbed my keys and walked out the door, this time not shutting it. It wasn't like I was coming back again.

I forgot to decide on a place that I would do it. I wasn't looking to cause a scene, but I didn't want to sit there for weeks before someone found me either.

The only place that made any sense was the lake. People came there every day, but it was never too crowded when Danielle and I would go there. It'd be perfect.

I got in my car and put in my favorite CD, Jay Z's *Reasonable Doubt* album, and turned the key. It was low on gas as usual, but had just enough to get me to the destination.

On the way there I could hear everything from last night as if it were playing through the speakers instead of the lyrics I was listening to. Seeing Danielle's face shedding tears I couldn't wipe away sent a cold pain through my chest.

I made it to the lake. It was empty and as peaceful as I'd ever seen it. Nobody was there since it was already early afternoon and classes were still in session.

I went to the only spot around the lake I knew, the one Danielle and I went to on our nights we had deep conversations to get to know each other. It brought back more memories and feelings that I could count on never having back.

No more wasting time. I popped the trunk and fetched for the pistol. Trying to figure out exactly where the bullet could be loaded was a challenge. I wasn't familiar with guns and forgot to ask for a manual, but I eventually figured it out.

I pulled out the pictures from our memory box to see them one last time. It was the last sight I wanted of my 22 year-old life, the good days when things were still the way it was supposed to be.

I grabbed the pistol firmly in my palm, now very sweaty, and placed my finger on the trigger. The gun was shaking so badly I had to pace my breathing. If I missed, I wasn't going to have another chance to do it right because I only had one bullet.

Closing my eyes, I put the gun in my mouth pointing it toward the roof of my gums, held my breath, and pulled the trigger....

click

The safety was still on. My heart was beating out of my chest, my shirt now drenched in a mixture of tears and sweat, and I felt myself getting ready to hyperventilate. I leaned my head back to the headrest.

I looked down at the gun and found the safety slider on the side and turned it off.

I couldn't mess up this time.

So I mustered up the courage to do it again. Still feeling myself getting cold feet, I started talking to myself.

"Damn you, Shawn, do something right for once," I whispered.

I put the gun back in my mouth aiming it the same way as before.

Eased my finger onto the trigger. Closed my eyes again and tears gushed out.

I stopped thinking, and started squeezing....

"SHAWN! NO! SHAWN!!!"

I opened my eyes and saw Danielle and Jazmin running full sprint to my car.

It Could All Be So Simple

I snapped out of memory lane and came back to Dr. Holley's office at the sound of her crying.

"Jesica?" I said. "Are you all right?"

"Yes. I'm okay," she sobbed.

I got up and walked around. When I spotted her bathroom, I went in and unrolled a few sheets of tissue before walking back towards her.

"Here, take this."

She grabbed them, trying to hide her face. "Thank you, Mr. Fletcher. Really, I'm okay. Just my allergies. I need to dust in here, that's all."

"Right...um. Do you want to just pick this up another time or...?"

She sniffled a few times, pulling herself together. "No, we can finish, but I want to say something before we do."

I sat back down on the couch and kept listening.

"Mr. Fletcher, I'm so glad you didn't hurt yourself, and thank you for being honest enough to share that. But I want to let you know, no matter what, there's always something to live for, even if you can't see it at the moment."

"I understand. Now I do. But, not every day you wake up feels like a blessing. As a matter of fact, it can feel like a curse. When you feel like you're living in hell, dying and taking your chances of going doesn't seem like such a bad idea. But I know better now."

"Right. Well I just wanted to put that out there, but there's no need to dwell on it for too long since that's not why you've come. So, I know you had mentioned something earlier about learning to forgive yourself. What's keeping you from doing that?"

"Well that's why I'm here. I don't think I'm a bad person, but I...I just-"

"Believed in something you couldn't live up to."

"Yes."

"Well, that doesn't make you evil. That makes you human."

"But society ain't tryna hear that. Neither is my ex,"

"To hell with society. I know, you're still considered a cheater, and in some people's eyes, that won't change for as long as you live. But that's a lot like saying a car is broken without diagnosing the root issues. On the surface, it makes sense, but that kind of limited thinking won't get you far. Society's motive is rarely to fix the problem, just a diagnosis that makes them feel better about the skeletons in their own closets."

"You ain't never lied, Jesica." I said in agreement. "But one more question; should I, or should I not try again at love? I mean, I know what I want, and that's a real relationship, a real marriage and a real family. But I can't wear the blood of another broken heart on my hands again. I simply can't."

"Well you don't have to. First you have to understand that there's a such thing as consciously doing something you know is wrong without intentionally causing the damage as a result. For instance, people text and drive all the time, but few intentionally plan on running off the road into a ditch. They knew that what they were doing was wrong, but they didn't anticipate the rest. The seeds of your actions were planted long before the fruit came along. To change your harvest, you have to change your seeds."

"English, please."

"Like your lack of communication. Where communication dies, assumption will thrive and trust won't have a chance to develop. You're not doing anyone a favor by lying. The moment you felt any physical attraction for Jazmin after you were in a committed relationship should've been your cue to discuss it with Danielle."

"So she could simply tell me to end my only real friendship? Not saying it wouldn't have been worth it, but what about the next attractive person. I mean, I can't go blind or go hide under a rock just so I can be in a relationship."

"But you can humble yourself enough to know that you're only human and that the women you have physical attraction for need to be kept at a distance before you lose what really matters; or rather, what matters most."

She closed her laptop and sighed, still staring at me as she gathered her thoughts for what she was about to say next.

"Mr. Fletcher, you're not that much different from a lot of my clients. You've spent most of your life trying to be something you're not; a bachelor and a player. You settled for those lifestyles thinking you could full-proof yourself from heartache. Those lifestyles develop safety nets we run to when we want to escape our reality; some people's safety net is drug abuse, yours was women, particularly, Jazmin. The place where you went wrong, where a lot of men and women go wrong, is when you tried to force your relationship while not being all the way healed from the past hurt. Up until the first break-up, you were all in. But afterwards, you subconsciously withdrew from the idea of 'relationship'. But you loved Danielle too much to see her go for good because you couldn't stand the idea of her being in the arms of another man. And because humans have the capability of being deeply in love while not being ready for a relationship, you dove head first into something you weren't ready for. That's why you crashed at the next sign of trouble."

"So basically, I should've cut my safety net from the beginning. But, I didn't want to for-"

"Fear of hitting rock bottom again once things fell apart. But, a part of being in relationship, is being brave enough to take that risk, and building a trust with your partner beforehand that gives you that courage, Mr. Fletcher. You can't adequately give Plan A a chance if you're always making sure there's a Plan B just in case things don't work out. I know you've always wanted something real, but pain molded you into something that wasn't ready for it when it came. However, you can use this pain you still have to get you back to where you need to be."

"Back to where I need to be? You mean, back to where I was before?"

"Yes."

"I don't mean to get all spiritual on you, but why would God put someone through so much just to bring them back to their starting point. I mean, I made the decision early to do the right thing but it's like He punished me for that. Just so He can get me back all over again? Come on man."

"First off, you have free will and made your own choices. So he didn't punish you for anything. But believe it or not, there are a lot of women who believe 'once a cheater, always a cheater'. It seems that now, God is wanting to use you as His proof of what He's capable of, even when dealing with a cheating man's heart. That's why He's given you the platform you have today to reach people. Nothing is a mistake, so long as you learn from it."

"And live to tell the story,"

"Yet here you are." she said smiling. "Well, let's stop and take a break. We can pick up later and continue the session another time. But I'm curious. How did Jazmin and Danielle come together to find you in your car? And you never told me who your ex is. It's been three years between now and the time you were at that lake, so are you referring to Danielle, or did you and Jazmin also have a relationship afterwards?"

My stomach rumbled, signaling lunch time. I looked at the clock and got the cosign I needed.

"Jesica, I think that's a great place to, as you say, *pick up later.*"

Made in the USA
Middletown, DE
22 December 2014